PHOENIX RISE TRILOGY

The Long Road from HELL
Book I

The Long Road From Hell

Copyright © 2019 by Stephen P. Miles

All rights reserved. No part of this publication may be reproduced, distributed, or transmitted in any form or by any means, including photocopying, recording, or other electronic or mechanical methods, without the prior written permission of the author, except in the case of brief quotations embodied in critical reviews and certain other non-commercial uses permitted by copyright law.

To learn more or find out when the next books are ready, follow the author or read my blog. Visit me at WWW.PhoenixRiseTrilogy.com (http://www.phoenixrisetrilogy.com/) You can also contact me through email at info@phoenixrisetrilogy.com

Tellwell Talent
www.tellwell.ca

ISBN
978-0-2288-0620-2 (Paperback)

Table of Contents

1. It Gets Cold Out There 1
2. Killer and Marex 15
3. The Tavern 28
4. To Hell with It All 49
5. We Are All Scared of the Darkness 64
6. Between Hell and High Water 90
7. Origon 121
8. The Sands of Time 134
9. Trinity 151
10. Cronus Prison 165

The Fall

The road to hell is quick and easy
The fall is added by gravity
With so many hands
To pull you down
Misery's only friend
Is the company it takes with them

1

It Gets Cold Out There

Hudson Bay space elevator June 23, 8142

"You did good work back there, Az," Mic said as he swiped the chip in his wrist. "Management will be happy with you."

They walked through the door. It was a typical looking office with a desk, some bookshelves, and a red light in one corner where Mic poured two scotches on the rocks at the little bar before sitting at his desk in the middle of the room. The only difference between this office and all others was that it was in the middle of the space elevator and the only office on it.

Mic opened the top drawer and threw an envelope across the desk from it.

"Forty thousand cash, and your papers are already uploaded for the life extinction program—another two hundred years."

Az looked at him with a half-cocked grin. "Pleasure doing business with you."

As he looked in the envelope, Mic leered over him from his seat.

"Welcome to the condemned."

"I have been here for a long time," Az said.

"That's a lot of time on your hands, Az. Perhaps one more mission before you retire. If successful, another five hundred years will be added to your life."

Az paused and looked back up at him with his hardened eyes.

"Is selling time the only thing you space boys have to barter with?"

"It's just the most effective way of getting things done."

"Well Mic, I'm over four hundred years old now. The first three hundred years I spent fighting in Earth's army on god forsaken rocks in space, and the last fifty freelancing for it. There's more to life than killing and sitting in a ship back and forth from it."

"You're right," Mic said. "There's a lot of space out there. You have two weeks to think it over. With five hundred years, you can make it all the way to the centre of the Milky Way. The end of the galaxy and the path of the gods."

Az raised his glass. "And I intend on seeing the pyramids of the ancient all the way there."

They clicked their glasses together and drank as a noise drew their gaze to the intercom.

—Now at Isaac Skyport. Two-day layover until the elevator commences its final ascent—

Mic and Az looked back at each other.

"That trip feels like it gets faster every time," Mic said. "I'll be taking the elevator with you, Az. When you decide to take on this next mission, let me know?"

Without another word, Az got up from the desk walked over to the door. As he opened it to leave, Mic spoke up.

"Everyone wants to go to heaven, but how many people get a chance to go to hell?"

He walked out onto the deck floor just in time to watch the thick glass panels open the elevator up to the skyport. It was the one stop the elevator made between the Earth and space while they tightened up and did a final inspection on the cables it would be riding on.

There was a huge superstructure built around the space elevator that added stability while it travelled. Then, at the top of the structure, it only rode on the cables to the space station. The cables not only hang down but also pushed up with an old Viking rope braiding design. There had been talk about replacing them with light beams, but there was too much at stake.

When the world faced its greatest fear of extinction from global warming, it was assumed that the glaciers and ice caps were what was keeping the earth cool (like ice cubes in a glass of water), so suction tubes were attached to the bottom of the cables and smaller ones ran in the middle of the wires where the water was suctioned up at Hudson Bay. The water also ran through the entire elevator and had a small electrical charge running through it. This created a magnetic field, making the elevator weightless so that the gears riding along the cable could bring it either up or down with ease.

In school one of the more fun science experiments was when they took a frog or a toad and levitated it via the water in its body. In doing so, it showed the kids how the elevator worked.

Then the water was connected at Space Station Isaac over the bay and would run along a protective shield of the Space Bridge known as Beta Moon. The water flowed along the outer shell of the entire space structure, and this allows everyone to be shielded from a gamma burst of the sun. Then the water returned to the Earth at Space Station Ismael in Antarctica and flowed along the Benguela Current—the only natural habitat of penguins, sea lions, and other cold creatures that were forced to migrate there. Their survival and that of the cold-water schools of fish that fed them required the slushy form of ice water that flowed there from it. All this kept the world at a perfect temperature and ensured a consistent flow of water through the South Atlantic Gyre.

After Earth first colonized Mars as a fully functioning support planet, mankind put volcanic ash into the upper wind current on Earth to create an artificial ice age that saved the planet from becoming a desert. After the three hundred year ice age, the nitrogen from the settled ash helped the Earth terraform itself back into a green and blue planet.

Az walked to the skyport bar windows and watched the jets landing and taking off as they flew over the North Pole carrying VIPs, diplomats, and royalty into Europe and Asia.

"The world must have been a different place when the North Pole was fully covered in ice glaciers," the man standing beside him said, his gaze fixed through the lookout window.

"Isaac and Ismael had saved some of it," Az replied, as he walked away, sat at the bar and ordered some soup and a beer.

For forty-seven hours he sat at that bar stool, sipping on whiskey and beer, only getting up to use the latrine. That was until he heard the words –*now boarding*– and walked back to the check in for the elevator. He swiped his chip, took his bunk number, and went to bed.

His slumber was rudely disturbed when he heard the voice of a young military police officer.

"Sir. Sir, wake up, Sir! You have been summoned to report to the master general's office."

He looked up at the two soldiers standing over him and only said, "So much for two weeks."

He wondered how long he had been asleep for as he rubbed his eyes with the palm of his hands.

His head was still in a haze and his eyes blurred over from the drink. The two MPs walked him over to the office door and stood on either side of it with their backs against the wall. Az scanned his chip on the door as it opened.

The master general was not there, however; only a box with the loyalist stamp embedded into it was on the desk. He poured himself a drink from a high shelf bottle then sat in Mic's chair and scanned the box with the chip in his wrist. As the top slowly opened, Az pulled out a red folder and scanned the first page.

> BY OPENING THIS BOX, YOU HAVE ACCEPTED YOUR MISSION. THE DOOR IS SEALED UNTIL THE CONTENTS OF THIS BOX IS RETURNED.

Az laughed out loud.

In the envelope, there were diagrams of the planet code named Hell, the space station they built on one of its moons, and the station they built connecting it to Earth's system. It showed how the planets in each solar system had planets that spun in the opposite direction and how it was always a retrograde planet that was connected to the next solar system by twin magnetic fields knows as dark matter (one above and one below) that spaceships could use like shipping lanes that would cut down on over half the travel time.

However, Earth's system only had one viable path—above it—as for the system below, it offered no means of return, nor did it connect to any other system. Earth was between two arms of the Milky Way and very disconnected from the rest of the galaxy, which was why Earth was never really visited other than by the gods when they found it, before the Hands of Time left. Or that was the story they knew, so far.

Az dug into the paperwork about the Hands of Time and how inside the Milky Way's black hole led to other parts of the universe. It was believed that at the Big Bang—the beginning of everything—started there inside of what would become known as the pendulum and spread across the nothingness, creating life, the universe, and galaxies that are all magnetically connected by dark matter. A constant tug of war existed between dark matter trying to pull it all together and dark energy trying to push it all apart and the black hole in the Milky Way leading into the bridge of all bridges, the Pendulum. No ship could cross this void when the Pendulum was not there, and the pressure of the black hole would tear anything apart. In the middle, there was one sun that burned so brightly it could only be fueled by heaven itself and a string of planets that stretched across it, connecting each tear into this universe together. Also, the reason no one could find one starting point of the Big Bang was because there were *many*, and like a clock's hand, the planets of the Pendulum spun so slowly across the beginning of all creation the closer you were to a black hole the slower time passed (conversely, the further you were from the pull of such a black hole the faster time passed).

Man was said to have been created by a Ship of the Gods on its way to hell to gather supplies and create a workforce before landing there. The purpose of that ship was unknown; however, the Ships of the Gods were believed to be the only ships capable of crossing the void between each solar system. Unlike the ships man had encountered so far, the gods' ships did not need the magnetic fields of each system to be able to get anywhere without the journey taking thousands of years. These magnetic bridges could always be found by the planet in a retrograde motion from all the other planets in the solar system. This was because, although it was caught in the gravitational orbit around its sun, it was also being affected by the dark matter stream of the other solar system it was tied to.

Az skimmed along the rest of the pages for a while until he came across a few points of interest. By the time the gods were done on Earth, humankind had spread across the entire planet and had gained knowledge that worried the gods—things like how to use their technology. They feared humankind might bridge the missing DNA needed to make humans gods themselves. When the gods left the Earth, they created an ice age on the planet that was meant to wipe out all of mankind; however, humans survived and evolved (or some think they devolved).

–The Mission

The gold army was created at the time of the first wars Earth had fought in the stars against the Takari. The rival species had been slaves to the gods and were left with their planet intact. So obviously they had a technological advantage over the earthlings. It was like a cornered housecat that figures out how to use a knife from the kitchen instead of just its claws.

So man created immortals to mimic the gods. They recruited the gold army. It was an army whose sole purpose was to defend the gold and other precious metals that were mined from Earth's solar systems asteroid belt. This army had only one recruiting need and one motto:

Stay alive and don't steal the gold.

The golden army was attacked by everyone, including each other, so they were the perfect ones for this mission. They were given heavy DNA-coping drugs and microbiotic treatments to alter their form, making them godlike. Except the gods were made of arsenic, and the touch of them was poisonous. The gods did not eat as all other life eats. They needed their food refined, and that was what all other living creatures were to them—refineries. The gods only drank the blood of the living in order to receive all the nourishment needed to live. Or at least that was as much as mankind knew about the gods back then.

So they created this army and turned them into bloodthirsty monsters then dropped them off on the opposing home world. The war ended quickly after that, and with no need for these soldiers, they were to be retired to the planet Hell. They were believed to still be alive there and had settled on an island called Origon, believed to be a tomb of a god. The golden army were Earth's best chance of gathering information of the gods. It was to be entrusted to Az to complete this mission and return with as much military intelligence as he could gather.

Az shook his head. *Military intelligence, now there is an oxymoron if I have ever heard one.*

He packed the files back in the box, watching the weight calculator go up as he put each file back in and sealed it shut by scanning his chip over it. Then he went to the bar in Mic's office and poured himself a few drinks of fine aged scotch.

When he walked out of the office, he saw the two MPs still standing at the door. They didn't move as he walked past them to the cafeteria and picked up a tray, grabbed some hard-boiled eggs, coffee, and toast, then sat down to watch the people power walk around the elevator.

The space elevator was a complete circle that people would walk to avoid the boredom of the trip. It was more like watching a dog tied to a pole. A dog will stretch its chain as far out as it will go until he is almost choking himself—and then stay at the end of it.

The rest of the elevator was pretty basic.

But in its time, I'm sure it was an amazing feat of accomplishment.

The design of it was stolen by the government from an engineer who was designing a new elevator to replace the old ones after four hundred years.

The cables it rode on were made of a synthetic plastic alloy with strands of spider web fibres to hold it all together. The spider silk proteins were extracted from the milk of genetically modified goats and were also used in the body armour of the foot soldiers as well. There were five cables that the elevator travelled on. They were spun in a spiral so tight it made the station above it have gravity slowing the spin of the Earth and adding an extra four hours to each day. From the spinning motion, it pushed the space station away from the Earth, so it was not sucked in by Earth's gravity. The cables were threaded, and the elevator had five gears that spun along them like a bolt to a nut, however, it only needed three to keep moving in case maintenance was needed. When the elevator reached the ozone layer that was the only time the rockets were used so that it could break through the three golden rings placed in Earth's ozone. Each ring was made of the purest gold taken out of the water in the ocean and created its own ozone layer to protect the Earth's atmosphere from the vacuum of space. The rockets were used until the elevator reached the outer orbit where the gears began to work again.

You see, original travel from Earth into space would punch a hole in the atmosphere, and every time it was done, it would cause a natural disaster whether it would be a flood, typhoon, hurricane, or tornado—it was always something catastrophic as the world corrected the balance.

–Now docking. Please return to your designated sections–

Mic was right, the ride does feel like it gets faster every time.

He went to gather his luggage and scanned his chip.

The baggage clerk said, "Sir, your luggage has already been brought to your room. Please enjoy your stay at Beta Moon Hotels on the Isaac Space Station."

Az sighed in annoyance. *There goes the cash.*

He stared at the sun for a minute through the thick tinted glass windows then went to his room to find the luggage there. He opened the case, and to his surprise, the 40k in cash was still there. He opened a safe behind the door, put the money in it, and scanned his chip as it took an ear print when it closed for the first time.

He sat on the couch and touched the screen on the coffee table.

—You have four messages—

A hologram appeared with the face of a beautiful woman leaning forward just enough so you could almost see her cleavage.

"Hey Honey! It's Mellissa, I heard you were back on the station. How about we go out tonight?"

Then two static messages, and one that showed the station and its luxuries *—Welcome back to Beta Moon Hotels, sir. For your convenience, we have made you two reservations for dinner to choose from—*

Az flipped through the virtual menus and selected the confirmation button at the bottom of one. Then he forwarded Mel the reservation.

He knew Mel could pluck the string of his heart like it was a harp, and if he saw her this long without being laid, she would play on his emotions as though he was a marionette.

He made one more reservation while pondering his next course of action as he nodded off until he had a craving.

Az opened the fridge and poured a bottle of beer into a glass then went back to the coffee table and called up Mellissa to leave a message on her machine.

"I have reservations at Don Shondey at seven. I hope I'll see you there. End message."

Then he went into the closet and took out one of the rental suits. In the upper-class apartments on the stations, there were suits and dresses in the closets that you could rent for the night. Of course, you paid for them as soon as they were taken out from the plastic. So if you tried on a couple to find one you like, it could get a little expensive. Especially, if your date didn't come back with hers, and Mellissa had a habit of walking off with a new dress every time she came to visit. As for Az, he always stuck with the black CK suit with a gray shirt underneath. It was the first thing he ever tried on, and he never tired of it.

He then went to meet Mellissa. He was, as always, right on time and found that she had already ordered a bottle of champagne and was sipping on some out of a flute. He walked over to the table without waiting to be escorted, and Mellissa stood up as he kissed her cheek then waited for her to sit again before seating himself. Az stared into her eyes without saying anything. He could see the age beginning to form around them and the memories of younger days in her eyes.

"Nice dress."

Mellissa smiled at him. "What this old thing? I've had it forever."

"Of course, Mel. How could I ever forget that weekend?"

Mellissa's wide smile turned into a grin. "You flatter me, sir. So how have you been?"

"Good," he said. "Still doing the army thing, and you?"

"I'm still in university."

"What's it been? Thirty years since I passed through this station last?"

She took a sip of her champagne. "About that, how was your vacation on Earth, did you go back home?"

"No, but it was relaxing nonetheless."

After dinner and a couple more bottles of wine, they stood up from the table as she held his hands with her small soft fingers and began to rub them with her thumbs.

"It was nice catching up with you."

"You know, Az, I am going to the Red Velvet dance club later if you want to meet me there? But then you're probably going to that shitty little bar you always go to, aren't you?"

"You used to work there if I'm not mistaken," he said.

"Yes, but some of us grow up."

"Sure," he said, "but none of us ever seem to grow old anymore, Mellissa. Who knows, perhaps I will see you at the club tonight."

"Perhaps," she said—then hugged him and walked away.

While he stood there watching her walk away, the waiter came over to scan Az's chip to pay for the dinner.

2

Killer and Marex

As predicted, Az went and sat down at a dark table in the corner of the old bar that had been there for as long as he could remember. The name over the door might change, but the bar always stayed the same. He sat at his table and drank his draft beer, staring at the empty bar until a group of soldiers came in for a drink. Two of the soldiers sat at the table beside him, continuing on in their conversation without even noticing he was there. The name tapes on their chests suggested their names (or at least handles) as Marex and Killer.

Marex was saying, "… and without the doses for life extension, I would have been dead at forty.

"Even farm boys like you live into their hundreds," said Killer.

"Yeah, but small hearts in my family. We die by the age of sixty at the most, unless we can save enough for the treatment or a new heart at the least."

"So, that is why you sign for the OFL?"

"Don't we all? Time served, time returned plus forty years for dying. The government does have it right, create humans in a lab and then have them choose to sign up to pay back the cost of living and schooling."

"Yeah, but you are one of those natural born kids. You had a choice," Killer said showing the barcode number on his arm.

"Why haven't you had that removed yet?"

"Why bother? Those numbers were my name until I joined."

"And, how did you get the name Killer anyways? A guy named Killer I figured would be a lot crazier than you."

"It was back in basic training, maybe someday I'll tell you. Between you and me I thought basic training was going to kill me."

Marex nodded. "Well, I swear my sarge tried both on Moon Base Alpha and Mars. So, were you trained in the dunes too?"

"Mars," said Killer. "All there is are sand dunes and factories. But better than training in the tunnels, they still haven't cleared them out yet."

"How do they consider that training anyway? Try to stay alive as long as you can in those tunnels while the creatures try and eat you or get into your mind with their nightmares.

Even if they were some kind of humanish things once, they aren't now."

Killer looked grim. "Yeah, well I sure was thankful for them when I was stuck, and those third-term BTLs saved my ass."

"Don't you know it, Bro."

From an intercom above the bar —*Now leaving orbit seven for orbit eight*—

"You don't believe in all that Buddha, Jesus, and Taoist crap, do you?" Marex asked.

"We are all part of one force, the blood of the Earth. How can you not believe in that?"

"They were completely different religions crammed into one for convenience."

"No," said Killer, "they were all the same religion viewed differently. Taoism was only taught to kings and the wealthy until Buddha, a prince, taught it to the common people, and Lao Tzu understood the books he was a caretaker for and tried to explain it to the people around him. Mohammed and Jesus are almost the same story, and both are traced back to sons of Abraham, and like stepbrothers, their religions fought each other for over two thousand years until the internet showed the youth they were both right and they stepped back from their fathers' fights. Anyway, I will meet you at the bar when we're done. Now scan your chip so I have your digits."

Marex scanned his wrist onto Killer's T2700 series armcomp—a mini computer that everyone had on their arm. A T2700 projected visions onto walls or tables or produced holograms depending on how much was spent on them. A person's whole life was dependent on the chip in their wrist for their information and money and their T2700 kept them plugged into everything. The only thing that was not allowed to be tied into the chip was a credit card. They were issued as cards and the sole responsibility of the credit card company for you to pay not the government's life chip.

"Take care, Killer."

"You too, my friend."

–Cannon Fodder (*Solar System #741*)

The battleships and carriers were at the edge of SS741 (planet Aha Rw) home of the Hurun people named for the first Earth ship that colonized it after crashing into the planet—the settlers mixed with the native humanoid species. In 4039 they became independent from Earth and had an embargo placed on them from the United Senate. They were not allowed to travel into space by orders of the senate and the pulse cannons that were found on their planet did not let any of the senate ships close to the planet.

The tension was so thick amongst all the ships of Earth's elite 2nd Armada it was as if they were walking through a muggy fog. The waiting burned inside the guts of every soldier there. They all knew the call was inevitable and the alarm would sound. The loyalists didn't bring that many ships for a peace negotiation.

Admiral Richardson was sitting in the captain's chair on the flagship USS *Salt Lake City*. He was a take-no-shit hard-ass said to be the protégé of General Blood and Guts, named because he believed he was the reborn general of a war long ago on Earth, and he sure showed he could win battles. If Richardson was there, then war was inevitable. The admiral had the senate on the front screen of the ship as they were determining whether or not to give the order. Sitting on the right arm of the captain's chair were four buttons and one red phone. The blue button was for engineering, the yellow was to prepare for defensive maneuvers and shields, the orange button was for the weapons rooms, and the red button was for attack.

You could see the boredom in the admiral as he sat there without saying a word, listening to the senate. Then as it sounded like the senate was going to call off the attack, you could see each member of the senate table push something on the table and the united senate's secretary of war stood up and picked up a large red phone on the wall. The senate room went on mute, and the red light on Admiral Richardson's chair blinked. He picked up the phone and pushed the red button and only said two words before hanging it back up: "Yes ma'am."

They already had been briefed on their drop zone, the coastal city of Tyre. They would take catfish, a modernized Higgins boat, and roll up onto the beach shore in them. The entire first wave was already suited up in military-grade space suits that allowed the soldiers to fight on land, underwater, and in space. There were thousands of different designs and companies that produced them. But the United Senate Military used the SACS 68 Petabyte (Space Atmosphere Controlled Suit). Marex just sat there staring at the floor as they waited in the warbirds, ready to drop. He couldn't get it out of his head how 65 percent of all first-wave troops were either killed or mined—but that first-wave survivors had an 80 percent survival rate through the first two years.

Then the alarm sounded, and the bars came down over the soldiers' suits as if they were about to go on a rollercoaster ride. Only this ride featured no exits on the other end. The battleships and cruisers made quick work of the outer solar system defenses. However, any cruisers that went into the system were destroyed in seconds.

Then the massive wave of warbirds began to rain down on the planet like fire falling from the sky. The warbirds had one objective, breach the atmosphere, drop the catfish (landing ships) into the ocean, and bomb the shore, using their remaining fuel to breach the orbit again and return to the carriers. However, if they couldn't make it back out of the atmosphere, they were to stay fighting and land on the landing strips the foot soldiers were to make or secure.

Marex was sitting beside the landing ship's driver, SlayDog, and could hear his conversation with the pilot.

SlayDog, this is BigBird, said the pilot. *We've been hit and are going down with you so prepare for a harder dive.*

"Roger that, BigBird."

I will release you at 10,000 meters.

"That's a negative, BigBird. I'm reading no breach in your hull, so we're taking you down with us, the bird's engine is in no shape to land on your own."

Roger that. 50,000… 40,000… 30,000… 20,000… Brace for impact.

Marex could feel the extra weight as his body shifted forward from the impact.

Well underwater as they began their climb, BigBird dropped all their bombs to lessen the explosion in case they were hit. The catfish were like submarines on wheels covered in a nanocoating to keep them waterproof and absorb any radar waves. No one inside could see anything until the doors opened, and no one was allowed to use their comps in case they could be picked up by the enemy. They would ride just under the waves until hitting the sand bank.

Once on the surface, BigBird's crew in the warbird looked skyward as the fighters that flew over them dropped their payload and created a wall of flames along the beach before blasting back out of sight. The boat drove up onto the shore, and the front doors of the ship pushed opened while the machine gunners tore through whatever was left alive in front of them.

The catfish was a basic design, not really changed since the twentieth century. They were the same length same width except they had a hard steel roof on them that allowed them to act as short-range submarines to reach the beach shore and the front would not fall open, leaving the entire crew exposed to oncoming fire. Instead, they pushed forward almost the entire size of the ship's length, leaving a wall in front of them with a hole for a machine gunner or rocket launcher to keep the soldiers covered. There was also a side hatch that could fall opened to allow any tanks or vehicles to launch from. When an entire beach was covered in catfish, it left a fortress along the shore while the fighter pilots destroyed all enemy artillery cannons firing on them.

The paratroopers would take strategic sites and Special Forces ops would secure important members of parliament. As learned in the second great war of Earth, it is not enough to take over the land—parliament must be secured first.

Marex ran out as number 12B from the catfish, and as soon as his foot hit the sand, the heads-up display, or HUD, a standard issue see-through computer screen equipped in every soldier's helmet picked up a sniper showing a 3D schematic of the building and all dark red dots inside as potential threats with light pink dots as civilians: building 35; 30th floor from the top; 7th window from the right—the red light started blinking as he zoomed in on its location, showing him the relay satellites were already in place.

The relay satellites showed all opposing life on the planet as red dots, the foot soldiers showed as blue dots, paratroopers as white dots, while the Special Forces could not be seen. Your own platoon was always shown in a different shade of blue than other crews in an amphibious assault, and on land mission it would be in green.

When the screen zoomed in on a target or showed a rally point or mapped locations, the HUD screen shaded out so that the soldier could still see if there was danger in front of them and had a rear camera view used more by video surveillance teams than the soldiers themselves. Marex steadied his gun and fired—the red dot grayed out and disappeared. A foot soldier's first job was to take out snipers, then machine guns, then the threat in front of them. While taking the shot, he took three hits in the armor, and after the confirmed kill, Marex returned fire on them.

The beachhead had a huge stone seawall that Marex assumed was for flood prevention. When they reached the wall, he could see some troops crawling into the sewers and Marex's HUD had a red arrow pointing to a path blown into the wall leading up into the city.

A picture appeared of Private Kim in the bottom left of his HUD, and when her lips moved he heard her say, *"Demo team must be taking the sewers."* He ran up the path behind some of his team only to be hit by the blast of an artillery cannon that threw him back onto the sandy beach.

When he came to, the tank teams were rolling up what was left of the wall.

"Sir. Sir, are you okay, sir? Hello, are you there?"

Marex opened his eyes to see a soldier with his T2800 plugged into his T2700. Then the HUD in his helmet rebooted.

"We have liquid solidified over the cracks in your armour," said the soldier. "You're back online and good to go."

Marex looked at the pieces of the foot soldiers left from the blast around him. The one thing the body armoured suits did was dehumanize body parts laying everywhere.

"Thanks, Doc."

"I'm an engineer. Get it right, Private."

"Yes sir!"

His screen began to flash a blue dot, then a map directing him to the rally point. He started jogging towards it and was happy as hell to realize his internal atmospheric control (IAC) was not damaged. It was an uphill jog the whole way, and he didn't break a sweat.

General Alta and Captain Hammerhead had positioned themselves on a cliff that gave them the perfect strategic viewpoint to overlook both the beach and the city of Tyre. Marex walked up the path towards them as he could see the faintest glimpse of the general's elite soldiers using their suits' camouflage mode, a setting that was too expensive to give to most soldiers. It took the image of the picture behind them and transmitted it in real time onto the suit. Even with a good trained eye, the only way to notice one of those suits was when a soldier walked in front of another one and it left a small half-second fade in the colour somewhere on the suit. Both the general and captain had their helmets off and were staring at the beach shore. Occasionally Captain Hammerhead would say something into his HUD.

"Just look at that shore," Hammerhead said, "the way the water leaves a red tinge on the sand with each passing wave.

"It reminds me of a poem back home," Alta said then looked out over the water as he recited it from memory.

"Hope floats up through a sea of blue

The bubble pops as it reaches the top

The last breath of hope from a dying man

Hopelessly sinking to the bottom

Now is floating in a northern wind

Lost is the man that never was

Now is no more."

"Beautiful, sir," said Hammerhead.

General Alta turned back to his captain. "Have the hovercrafts released, loaded, and armed for convoy by zero one hundred hours. Let's keep all soldiers time synced to Earth's twenty-eight-hour clock.

"Yes, sir."

Hammerhead turned and addressed him.

"Marex, you are receiving a field commission to sergeant. Take Foxtrot-6 and notate the bookstores and toy stores of everything."

"The libraries and colleges too, sir?"

"Are you retarded, soldier? You have your orders."

Marex's HUD lit up, and four dots in yellow started blinking and coming towards him as it changed design to sergeant mode. He used his T2700 to scroll through as much info as he could about his new squad. Their last sergeant was killed by a sniper, and the rest of his team was moving to the city's edge, taking up defensive positions.

When the troops arrived, they saluted. Marex addressed them.

"Soldiers, you have all been briefed for you mission on the way here."

"Yeah," said a soldier identified on the HUD as KillJoy. "We are collecting Barbie dolls."

"That's right, now let's move."

They scanned the books that were on display, and any military books they could find. Then they moved on to a nearby toy store.

While working through the aisles, KillJoy turned to another squad member identified as GutPunch.

"I can understand the bookstore, but why the toy store?"

Marex broke in over the com. "Because children's toys reflect adult life and things that have happened in the past of a society. Look at these toy animals, the ones with the fence in the package are obviously the farm animals and these ones with trees must be forest animals. In the five minutes it took to photograph this store, we already have a basic idea of their entire society and culture."

Then their HUD lit up: Foxtrot-6 was to meet up with Kilo-4, Bravo-2, and Golf-2, 3, and 9 in sector orange. Marex touched the release button on the keypad, and his squad received the info.

"Double-time it, team! I want my whole squad on the hovercraft in forty."

The hovercraft then landed on the street in front of Marex, where he and the four soldiers climbed in first. The craft picked up the rest of his squad, and they were dropped off in front of a small town in the middle of some farmer's fields that stood at the edge of a forest three times the size of Earth's Amazon rainforest.

The town was subdued quickly—the soldiers mostly used sleeping gas and stunners, for it is never the intention of a soldier to kill a farmer or any kind of civilian. After taking the town, they poured the rubber-tarmac out, and created an airfield where the warbirds began to land on.

3

The Tavern

Marex was playing dice with some of Foxtrot-6 when a group of fighter pilots came in after completing a bombing run. He couldn't believe it when he saw who was with them.

"Killer," he said, "if you'd talked any louder, the whole planet would know our location."

When the pilot saw Marex, he broke out in a big smile.

"Holy shit, look at you," Killer said. "A fucking sergeant now! Well, that's it, we've lost this war."

Killer sat down at their table. "I do believe last time we met it was your turn to buy."

"Oh no, good sir. It is truly yours."

"Why with manners like that," Killer said, "how could I not?"

A few hours later, the MPs came in and cleared the place out so the captains could drink. Marex and Killer went to sneak out the back door through the kitchen, hoping to grab some food on the way out when Marex noticed Captain Hammerhead.

"Sir, Killer and I here are going to sneak off down to the wine cellar and have a few more nightcaps."

"That's fine, Sergeant," Captain Hammerhead said. "Just make sure you're up by 0600. We are doing our assault through that jungle and into Riyadh to take out those atmosphere cannons."

The next thing Marex knew, he was lying face down on a dirt floor. Without moving his head, he could see Killer unconscious among a half dozen empty wine bottles.

"Killer, wake up. We're late. They're going to have my stripes for this."

Killer, still passed out, leaning against the wall, only opened one eye—probably because he was unable to open the other one yet—then closed it again. Marex peeled himself off the floor and wiped the dirt chunks from his face. He looked around at the small wine cellar with wood shelves and glass bottles. There was enough daylight coming through the floorboards that he could see everything clearly through the streaks of dust. That is he would've been able to see everything clearly, were it not for his hangover. He walked over to a small staircase almost like a ladder on the opposite wall that led to a hatch in the ceiling and for the life of him he couldn't remember descending it the night before.

"Killer, get up, you lazy shit and help me. This fucking door is jammed shut."

Killer moaned as he pushed himself up off the wall and walked over.

"Here, let me help."

They pushed on the hatch door trying to open it, and their blood started pumping to their heads, which throbbed mercilessly as a result. Killer groaned.

When they finally got the hatch opened, Marex watched as Captain Hammerhead's body rolled off of it—his bloody lifeless eyes meeting his. The tavern was pure carnage.

They didn't just shoot them, they beat them until they were dead.

"Holy shit," said Marex. "Everybody's dead."

"And I don't think those are our guys coming this way!" said Killer. "Quick, shut the hatch."

They stood there on that ladder without moving a muscle. The enemy soldiers walked on the floor over them while they both watched dust fall between the cracks, floorboard creaking with every step. One soldier stood right on the hatch and said something indistinct to his companions before they walked back out the door. Right away, Marex and Killer jumped off the ladder, and Marex looked at his T2700.

"There are reports coming in from all over, of the enemy pushing back."

"Check the back records," said Killer, "and see if you can find out what happened. As soon as they pass the building, I'm going to do a little recon."

Marex shooed him away with his hand and put on his helmet to try and find some videos of the battle. Killer stalked up the ladder, and just before he went through the hatch, he looked down at his buddy.

"Eh, I think we should keep radio silence," he said, "in case they have our frequency."

Marex tapped the side of his helmet and gave Killer the finger. Killer put on his own helmet and closed the hatch. Marex could hear him slide Captain Hammerhead's body back over top of it.

A few hours later, Killer returned and climbed down the ladder to find Marex with his sidearm pointed at him.

"I've counted fifty maybe a hundred troops," he said. "And with that tropical storm, we are practically invisible."

Marex said, "They've turned off all transmissions in this sector, so we are blind as well. But don't worry, I have an idea."

Killer sat down with his back to the wall beside Marex and pulled the cork out from a bottle of wine with his teeth and took a sip, while Marex showed him the map of the town he'd drawn on the floor.

Killer put corks where the enemies were stationed, and together they drew out the plans of how they were going to take it back over.

A day later, the hover tanks rolled into the town and their comps turned back on the screens displaying: CHIP RECOGNITION: COMPLETE ACCESS GRANTED...

Killer and Marex were standing on either side of the street when the lead tank stopped and opened its hatch. They were now back on the grid.

Over the helmet speakers came the voice of the driver and a small pic of her in their HUD.

—When I saw the two blue chips, I didn't know if I should say anything or not. But you boys look in fit shape to me—

The foot soldiers all jumped off the tanks and began to comb the town while the tank captain, a man by the name of Wahlberg, began to question Killer and Marex.

The debriefing was cut short, however, by a voice over the headset

—Sir, I think you should come take a look at this. Over—

"What is it?" asked Wahlberg

—You got to see it to believe it—

Wahlberg, Killer, and Marex walked into the tavern where sixty-eight soldiers had been captured and tied to the chairs positioned around tables. The tank captain looked at Marex who shrugged.

"Well it took you guys so long to get here, we needed some drinking buddies."

The soldiers began loading up all the supplies from the tavern into the tanks.

Wahlberg said, "With their artillery cannons bombing the beach, we can't use it even if we were able to take it back."

"Yeah," said Killer, "and it looks like they're using scorched earth on the farmland."

Pointing to the smoke and dim light in the distance, even with the rain falling.

"We're turning off all tracking beacons and hiding in the jungle," said the captain. "We don't have enough power to take the metropolis."

They hopped on a tank rolling past and watched the flashes of lights inside the tavern from gunfire as they rolled into the dense jungle.

–MOTMFJ

The tank crew stopped in a large clearing beneath two trees and ordered the tanks to circle wagons. Then the troops began to offload everything they had piled on them. A soldier working with Marex looked over at him.

"I don't understand how you guys did it. How did you take over the town?"

"Don't know myself," Marex said. "It was as if there were someone watching us, guiding our moves so that we could anticipate the enemy before they acted."

Captain Wahlberg walked over and stood between them. "Look, you have all the time in the world to be a hero when we get out of the Middle of the Mother Fucking Jungle, but for now finish propping up those huts."

The huts looked like they were flat skids stacked on top of each other and placed on spikes drilled into the ground. Then with a motor, they would crank them up to create a room and the floor pushed out at the bottom on the ones that were to be washrooms or kitchens to hold water underneath. There was even a hose with a pump and filter to put down a well, and in a jungle, it did not take long to dig for water. The roofs featured integrated high-yield solar panels in case of a deployment where no other source of electricity was available and could be rolled up in the case of stacking two or more on top of each other, which in this case, they were doing.

They had swept the clearing of all small trees and brush and used them to make a defensive border wall around the entire camp—more to keep the local fauna out than repelling an enemy offensive. Most of the troopers didn't wear their suits because they weren't allowed to use the on-board comps anyways. But the cameras stayed rolling.

The cameras *always* stayed rolling.

Two weeks later, an enemy chopper flew overhead. Everyone just stood there looking up and listening to the noise of air hitting the leaves on the trees as it passed. Marex looked down when he noticed a soldier had approached him on the guard wall they'd built.

"Sir, the captain would like to see you."

Marex walked with the soldier into the war room where there were two large metal tables. One with a diagram of the world, then next to it the metropolis known as Riyadh that had two atmospheric pulse cannons that were shooting into orbit and a dozen Howler artillery cannons firing onto the beach.

Anytime gunpowder was used in an artillery cannon they were nicknamed howlers from the noise they made when fired.

Marex shot the captain a crisp salute. "Captain."

"Well son, this mission seems to be in your favour. We are promoting you."

"I'm sorry, sir. I'm already sergeant. If I am promoted any higher, I will not be able to fight with my troops."

"Understandable son," said Wahlberg. "Then you will lead India platoon on our final assault attempt on the cannons."

"I will be honoured to, sir."

As they walked over to the table showing the layout of Riyadh, the captain explained how most of the troops retreated back onto the ships, which were waiting on the ocean floor to resurface.

"There are three stages to this mission, and only a handful of people know this. We were the first wave in on an amphibious assault. Then regardless of success, in twenty-one days, there would be a second land descent of reinforcement troops on the other side of Riyadh to cut off the enemy's escape. Then on the thirty-second Earth day, is drop day code name D-day. They will launch the entire second elite Earth armada at this planet. Do you know what that means son?

"Yes, sir," Marex replied

"Well, just to be sure, let me remind you. Whether armed or not, a caravan is a group of ships a hundred or less. A fleet of military ships is anywhere between one hundred to a thousand ships. That sitting up there is one of Earth's finest armadas, and I can assure you, son, there is more than a thousand and one, and all of those ships will be entering within range of those pulse cannons on D-day do you understand?

"Yes, sir."

Good son, then you know that Admiral Richardson will not put a single one of his shiny ships in danger if he does not have to. So if, by the thirtieth day, we have not secured those pulse cannons firing at his ships, he will use the railguns and launch a kinetic bombardment dropping enough rods to not only wipe out the entire metropolis of Riyadh but everything that surrounds it as well.

In three days, we will have been in this god dammed place for three weeks. So in eight hours, you are to have your troops loaded onto the tanks, and we will blow through this jungle using an old irrigation stream dating back to when this was all farmed and in that way attempt to get behind Riyadh. If this mission is not a success, they will drop those rods, annihilating everything. Do you understand? We need this mission to succeed and timing is everything."

"Yes, sir!"

"Dismissed, Sergeant."

Marex went outside to gather his men and ran into Killer, working on a tank engine.

"So, what's the word, Marex?"

"We leave first light for the final assault before they use the railguns on the planet."

"So they're really going to do it, eh!" said Killer. "They're going to blow up this whole planet to get those pulse cannons even if they're in pieces."

"Why don't they just steal the plans for them?"

"You should know," Killer said. "You were the one in the toy store. They don't know how they were built. The cannons were left behind from a war long ago. Long before we ever knew space existed."

"You have a far-out imagination, Killer. But after this mission, I quit drinking."

Killer laughed. "Quitting drinking is easy. I've done it a thousand times."

"See you on the other side."

"You too, bro. Take care now."

Marex put on his SACS 68. The HUD was not connecting to the satellites, but it was still linked to the T2700, and they had it set to analog with the suit antennas. That way they could communicate comp to comp.

He debriefed his men with all the words on the screen that were not in red. Marex knew all the men could see were the words in black as Killer stayed behind and stood at the door of the armoury watching the troops arm up. For some reason it was his favourite sight before a battle.

The soldiers were loaded onto the tanks as they ran through the puddles, mud dripping off their 68s. Once all the yellow dots were on the orange outline of the tanks on his HUD—along with the blue ones from all the other squadrons—they shipped off.

The rain dripped from his HUD.

Marex heard some static over his com, then Captain Wahlberg came through on a private channel.

—If they don't launch the next wave, our only form of backup will be ten days away, thirty or more if they walk from the beach. It's all or nothing, and they're not going to be picking us up if we lose, so make every shot count—

The crew sitting on the side of the tanks started singing as if they were in a bar. Before he stepped foot on Aha Rw, Marex would have probably sang along, but he knew what the words in red said. He'd seen them as he was reading the script to his men. It might as well have read:

ALL THOSE WHO ARE HERE ARE DAMNED, AND ALL THOSE WHO ARE DAMNED ARE ALREADY DEAD

But he had no idea just how true that was.

The jungle was so dense and thick you would swear you were going in circles. The tanks hovered over the overflowing waterway. Useless if they had to use the 90mm. A hovertank had to be on its treads to fire anything due to the force of kickback from the blast. But its .50 calibre machine guns were quite effective in getting through the jungle, and they lost a couple of men to what could only be described as a prehistoric alligator that could stand six metres tall when it attacked. It lay at the bottom of the river as the tanks passed over it then it grabbed one of the soldiers who had their feet hanging over the side of the tank and dragged her to the bottom. The troops started shooting in the water and screaming all at once so you could not understand what they were saying. Marex silenced the noise from his team's HUD and asked them if anyone knew what was going on back there.

—I think they saw a fish, sir—

Then Marex heard Captain Wahlberg tell Captain Monroe to move onto the shoreline

—*No can do, Wahlberg, these banks are too slippery and steep to use the tank treads to get out of here with. What did your surface rats see?—*

—*Some kind of alligator is under the tanks. You might want to get your machine guns prepped—*

As soon as Marex heard that, he ordered his troops on the turrets just as the beast stood in front of the tanks, knocking the lead tank back into the one behind it. One soldier held the 90mm as everyone else pilled on the turret and kept their head down as the .50s tore through its chest and exploded as they penetrated. The tracers were set every tenth round, and Marex counted three every second from the machine gun he was looking down on.

By the time they got out of the jungle, they knew why the enemy never went into it after them. If a planet could be considered alive, then the jungle would be its digestive track.

The tanks hid back on the edge of the jungle so that their locations could not be zeroed in on, and under the cover of the night, a hundred thousand troops snuck across the two days' worth of flat fields. During the daylight, they had lain perfectly still as the camouflage of their suits mimicked the grassy surroundings, making them almost invisible. The standard SACS 68s had a dozen pre-set settings: solid black, white, navy blue, red, yellow and gray that could also be added into the more advanced settings of jungle, desert, grassland and forest.

The wall to Riyadh was not there to defend the city from foreign invasion, but from whatever indigenous threat lived in that jungle.

When the attackers were only a half day from the wall, the defenders opened fire, and the tanks made quick work of the artillery cannons bombing the beach. That was the easy part, since the Hurun never stopped bombing the beach, the tanks had an easy time zeroing in on their location. Then the tanks opened fire on the wall, and heavy firefights erupted. They didn't break through until the sky fell, and the wall became a ragged line of rubble and flames. Marex knew some of their pilots had combed the city, waiting to drop their payload off on that wall. Most of the fighters never even made it.

Marex stopped his platoon at the wall and watched the fighters break out of the atmosphere. That was how he knew his battle had started again—and so did the rain.

What he didn't know was that Special Forces had succeeded in infiltrating the government and had the Hurun army scrambled across the city. They linked their screens again with the recon satellite, and it showed that their hovercopters were picking up the catfish on the beach.

That's when Marex's remaining forces received their orders. They were to take control of the atmospheric pulse cannons at any cost so that the battle cruisers could orbit the planet and make quick work out of this war.

Whoever controls the heavens controls the land.

They broke into two groups, and the satellite linked Marex up with one squad to take out Lima cannon while the other squad took out Papa cannon. Easier said than done. Special Forces might have scrambled the army, but their commander in charge of the cannons was not fooled at all.

Marex broke his squad of two thousand into ten teams as they reached the hill of the cannons while he barked orders into his microphone

"Team two I want you in front of the doors. Teams five and seven, I want suppressive fire along the roof. Shield teams, you are first in and hold the door for the ladies."

The shield teams were groups of twenty soldiers that worked like a Roman legion, covering the assaulting side of the troops. The first row of soldiers covered the front and the row behind them held their shields above like a roof. The shields were made of an electric graphite and built right into the left arm of their SACS 68AS (armoured specialty). When not in use, you could almost not even tell they were there since, without the shield activated, they were only a small round bar extruding from the arm—but fully extended, they were six feet tall and three feet wide. They also reflected the image behind them while the computer program removed any of the troops from the projection. At the same time a system known as the Golden Eagle projected everything in front of them onto the back of their shields. This way, there were no cameras that could make it easy for the enemy to identify the shields. They marched up the hill behind the shields as the bullets fell to the ground, showing little round dots like water falling into a puddle when the Hurun bullets hit the shields. Their machine guns spread so much metal, it was like trying to walk on round rocks.

As they entered the buildings—massive structures that were taller than any super structures on Earth—the hovercopters were dropping the catfish along the city's edge while some of the beach crews where linking up with Marex to compensate for the heavy losses. The 68s could withstand most of the small arms, but the laser fire chewed through it like they were plastic soldiers.

"Sir, I am reading a thousand Hurun coming down the hall under us."

"Detonate explosives into the floor," Marex said.

The explosives dropped a large chunk of their floor onto the Hurun soldiers below while Marex's force hid in a side room. Then 'bouncing betties' were tossed into the hall, and when they hit the ground, the grenade opened and shot up into the air two feet and sent waves of deadly military grade polymer beads across the hall. The force of those beads would tear through the enemy, and ricochet off any hard surface, turning anything in their path into ground beef.

Marex stationed two men over the hole and ordered the procedure repeated on every second floor they secured while his team climbed the building.

Then came an explosion so powerful it almost shook the whole building apart. Inside the structure, they had limited radio, so it wasn't until it was all over that they found out the other cannon had been overrun and that Papa-team had blown it up rather than losing it back to the Hurun.

They climbed that vertical maze, and every floor they had fewer and fewer troops, and the Hurun came at them with more and more of theirs. By the time they reached Lima cannon's commander, there was only Marex and a young private named Bode left. Getting into that room was almost impossible, for their suits were so damaged the plastic was sticking into their chests, and Marex had taken at least two shots to the shins. If he fell, he'd have been dead.

They had no grenades and were using seized Hurun weapons since they'd long ago run out of ammo.

Then they caught a break.

Two live grenades rolled up under their feet, and they were able to scoop them up and throw them back at the resisting force, killing them all. Marex ran at the door, pumping Hurun rounds into it, and when he hit it, he broke through tumbling to the floor. Private Bode fell beside him not even a second later. They looked at each other for a split second and then scrambled to their feet.

It looked like they'd crashed a Christmas dinner. There was a huge table under a crystal chandelier with a red tablecloth on a table that could fit twenty-five high ranking officers easily. There was even violin music playing on an antique priceless phonograph. The room had huge windows, and they could see the battle still raging below. The commander of Lima cannon was a gray-haired man with a long white beard sitting at the head of the table. Behind him was a fully stocked bar and a bartender who looked so pale Marex thought he was going to faint. Then the commander stood up and put his hand out in front of him. At his belt there hung a sword in an ornate gilt scabbard. To capture the cannon was the mission, to capture the captain would be the prize that could turn the table of the war.

As though Marex rehearsed it a thousand times he spoke up. "Sir, you are under arrest by orders of the United Senate. Will you comply with us?"

"Of course, I do young man, but it seems we have nowhere to go. If you take me out of this room, they will not only be shooting at you but me as well, and you look in no shape to take another hit. And so will you not join me for dinner at the least? I suspect my guests will no longer be arriving."

They had their guns pointed at him ready to fire until Marex put his hand over Bodes' barrel and eased it to the floor. Then he went to sit on the other side of the table to face him.

"No! No!" said the commander. "Do not sit over there, how will I ever hear you with my old ears?"

Marex nodded to Bode, and they sat closer. Marex sat to his left side and Bode to his right. The commander had a small sidearm sitting on the table; it looked like an old Luger—but with the shape of their 68s, Marex knew they wouldn't stop it. He took off his helmet and gloves as Bode did the same.

"Care for a drink?" the commander asked.

"Yes," replied Marex as Bode sat quietly.

"I am Commander Arkalane," he said as he snapped his fingers and the bartender brought over a bottle of wine as his hands shook. He spilled some pouring it into the glasses.

"Careful now, that wine is ten thousand dollars a glass. Now please eat."

"I am Sergeant Marex and this is Private Bode."

Marex cut into the roast beef and could see the blood run from it. His mouth watered while he served himself corn, potatoes, and peas and looked over at the commander and remembered when his father served a big dinner. He always handed the first plate to his grandfather who sat at the head of the table. Marex passed the first plate to the commander then to Private Bode and finally took the rarest piece for himself.

"Private Bode," the commander said. "Would you kindly pass the gravy?"

Marex could see Bode was shaky. The private kept staring at the gun on the table. After living on army rations and space slop for so long, that meal almost made him forget what was going on outside. They finished the plate, and the bartender brought over a plum brandy that they drank well eating hot apple pie and vanilla ice cream. Marex wanted to talk to him, wanted to say something, wanted to know what was going on in his head. But every time he opened his mouth, no words would come, so he just kept eating. That was until the commander stood up.

"I believe you have come here for this," he said and put his sword on the table. "Here is my official surrender, but would you not have a scotch with me first?"

Marex stood and walked over to the bar with him. The commander produced a couple of cigars, handed one to Marex and lit them with wooden matches, saying that the wood flame keeps from ruining the flavour of the cigar. The bartender poured two scotch on the rocks—the smoothest tasting scotch Marex ever had. Then the commander walked over to the window, and he and Marex looked out at the bodies lying on the hill and the thick dark smoke everywhere.

Marex looked at the old man and found the words to speak. "How did you build these cannons?"

"We did not build them. They came from the time of the great collision long before our gods were ever gods."

"How long ago was this?" Marex said staring into his eyes.

There has only ever been two great collisions, the collision of life and the collision of war. These came at the second great collision.

"So how long have you been the keeper of this artifact?"

"I have taken care of this cannon my entire life," said the commander. "That sword was passed down to me by the last person who held this post and who did not give it up until his dying breath."

Just then, the private yelled across the room.

"The gun, sir. It's missing from the table."

Without thinking, he turned to Bode, his instincts dulled by scotch and cigar smoke. He whirled back around and saw, for an instant, the face of the commander. Then with the pull of a trigger it was gone. His blood sprayed Marex in the face.

—

"It's all there in my report, council."

Marex looked at the seven members of the military tribunal for the loyalist union. The courtroom did not have an empty seat in it. The proceedings were packed with uniformed officers.

General Nathan Cain, head of the tribunal, said something under his breath to the colonel to his right then addressed Marex.

"And can you confirm that your testimony, that of your troops, and the video footage we have seen is all true and accurate?"

"Yes, sir."

"Everything seems to be in order," said Cain. "But what we don't have is exactly how, out of over a million people on the mainland before our final assault, only you and one raw private survived. Without those cannons being taken out, we never would have gotten our ships close enough to have taken the mainland. You are dismissed back to your quarters."

Two MPs walked Marex back to his room where he stood there looking out the small portside window at the chaos the pulse cannon had wreaked on the armada. He did not sleep. He just watched as builder ships tugged the two halves of a battlecruiser back together and began to weld it.

All he could think of was how, if he had accomplished his mission sooner, that ship probably wouldn't be in two.

The next morning, Marex was brought back to the courtroom and stood in front of the tribunal.

General Cain brought the room to order. "Sergeant Marex, is there anything you would like to say before sentence is passed."

"Thank you, sir," he said. "But I am ready for whatever sentence is deemed proper."

He said this, knowing that it could be an execution.

"Very well then. Sergeant Marex, number 350-4950-5488-4334-4, after careful deliberation and review, all charges against you of the unsanctioned assassination of the surrendered prisoner Commander Arkalane are dismissed. You are, instead, to receive the Medal of Valour for your work during the Hurun War. As well as a university course of your choice on Earth. A hero does not just prove himself in battle, but in the classroom as well.

4

To Hell with It All

Back on the other side of the galaxy, Az climbed out from his crashed ship and kicked it.

Goddamned government-issued piece of crap. How the fuck am I supposed to get off this planet now?

Then he picked up a plaque that had broken off from the side of the ship saying USS *Spirit* and tossed it like a Frisbee.

Fuck.

The field around him was dark, only illuminated by the moons overhead and some small fires that the ship caused when it crashed. He looked at the trail of parts it left and the broken-down treetops from his descent. Then his gaze turned back to the smoldering wreckage of what was left of the ship. Finally, he checked his T2700 to see the rest of the crew blinking white (dead).

With no recon satellite able to break through the atmosphere of the planet—and without someone to talk to comp-to-comp—the computer was useless as a communicator, but he just couldn't live without it. It could come in handy for maps in the database, recognizing edible plants, fish, or animals, what to do if bitten, if the water was drinkable, radiation in the area, translating someone's conversation, or at the very least playing a video game to kill time. After all, the T2700 was probably the only real friend a soldier ever had, and he loved the sound of the sexy voice he had programmed on it since basic training. Besides, he already had all his favourite porn downloaded onto it, and boredom leads to masturbation, masturbation leads to relaxation, relaxation leads to clear thinking, and clear thinking leads to strategic planning.

He walked over to the pilot's chair and looked at the blood dripping down the pilot's face from the broken glass that had shattered into both the pilot and the co-pilot. Whatever they hit, they hit it hard, that glass had been meant to withstand an asteroid impact. He grabbed the briefcase behind the captain's chair, took off his helmet, and looked around for the direction he should choose.

He drew his sidearm when he noticed a figure standing in the path of the crash. The silhouette of the figure was lit up by one of the fires, and he rested the sidearm back into his holster when he saw that it was an old man in a robe using a tree branch as a staff. Az walked up to him and greeted him using an ancient form of human dialect known as Demotic, a common language used on the planet.

"You are far from strange, but so strangely far from home," the old man replied as Az walked closer.

"It is odd to hear a man speak in ancient Greek?"

"Our first words," said the old man, "and those are what you choose?"

"I will strive to present myself in a more intellectual manner while in your presence. I am Az."

"And I am Nagi," he said. "To strive is to be smart. To be smart you create intelligence. Intelligence allows you to adapt to your surroundings, but knowledge allows you to adapt your surroundings to you."

"I am merely here seeking truth."

"Truth is a lonely thing to know. To seek truth, you must first separate yourself from everyone you know, and even if you wish to return to those people who now do not know, you would find yourself alone among them. However, the Pendulum of Time has not made its full return, so how did you get here?"

"It's a one-way trip to hell," said Az.

"Limbo is our sentence, and it will be lifted when the Pendulum returns."

"So, there are others like you?"

"Oh, yes! We are many. It seems the gift of immortality has been lost on you. We are marked 999 for every thousand years one is born again. That is the sign of the immortals of our kind. Forever it spins until they return again."

"That is who I am seeking, the immortals known as the golden army. They landed here a long time ago. That is my mission, I must find them."

"I know of who you speak," said Nagi. "But they are by no means yet immortals. They are on the Island of Origon. That is where they landed, and that is where you should try first."

"So, this is not Origon?"

"No, this is the mainland known as Asphodel, and you have crashed in the Elysian Fields."

"They overshot my landing," Az said. *What a bunch of useless fucking morons. I can't believe it—*

"The fates are what brought you here. They know what is right, not you."

"Fates or not, I must complete my mission."

"Spoken like a soldier late for his own funeral. This world is a dangerous place during an eclipse. When the moons are done gathering, you should pass then."

"An eclipse?"

"Yes, the planet's day and night while facing the sun are set by the moons that block the sun. Most only block it for a short period of time, enough to rest, and during this eclipse, the night caused by the moons' shadow will last for many years."

"Then I will travel at night."

Nagi raised an eyebrow. "This is a planet that is so big and spins so slowly that when it does not face the sun, night lasts for four hundred of your Earth years, and that is when the creatures of the night all come out to feed. With the night being as long as it is now, the small ones will be out looking for food, and you will not last past the forest's edge. Even if you do make it to the coast, how will you travel across the ocean to the island with no ship?"

"I am sure I will find a way, Nagi." Az gripped the handle of his case tighter.

"If you wish to weather this eclipse here, I will take you to the docks and help you charter a ship when it has passed."

"Thank you, sir. I will be glad for the help," Az said as he turned to head back to what was left of his ship.

"You are welcome to join me in my sanctuary. Perhaps you might find what you are looking for in an apple?"

Az stopped and looked back at the old man. "Well, I am kind of hungry. You're on."

As they walked into the treeline, Az looked up at the large moon's glow. "So how long do you think this night will last?"

"It is hard to say. The moons are always moving positions as they rotate around the planet. So they are never the same ones. From the markings on it this could be either Achlys or Nyx. If it is Achlys, the night will last for five years, and if it is Nyx the night will last for twenty years."

"Let's hope it is Achlys then," Az said.

Nagi only shook his head as he looked down and tapped his walking stick on the ground. A beautiful green glow spread beneath their feet. Az didn't even notice they were standing on a rock path until it lit up.

They followed the green illuminating glow to a small stone hut with a grass roof. The doorframe was made of stone, and it had markings on it. Az looked at the symbols: on the top right, the Big Dipper, the middle top stone a star (perhaps the North Star seeing as the Big Dipper's handle was pointing to it). However, the Big Dipper was a circle of stars with a point on the end, and it has not looked like that since the start of mankind from Earth?

What was it doing all the way here, and how old was this person? He remembered walking through a museum on Earth and seeing a copper tablet with the same marking of the Big Dipper on it.

Maybe this guy is from Earth, one of the soldiers. Perhaps they all went a little stir crazy down here. Then again, I see no fangs.

Nagi opened a wooden door held together by two black iron hinges and rivets.

They walked through the threshold and down a stone staircase into a large room with stone walls and a fireplace in one corner. The ceiling had wood rafters running along it held up by stone posts and three semi-round doors, one adjacent to the fireplace and the other two across from the staircase. The slight green glow of the rocks allowed Az to watch Nagi's movements.

As Nagi knelt in front of the fireplace, he lightly blew air out in a silent whistle, and with the movement of his left hand over the wood, a fire started, and the lanterns on the walls lit up as well.

"Cool parlour trick," said Az. "I have to learn that one."

"Fire is always there, behind existence. It is emptiness that can never be found. So by flint or force, it only needs to be summoned and fed."

"I understand."

Az and **Nagi** walked over to a bookshelf beside the stairs. It held stone tablets, scrolls, and leather folios. Above the shelf was a copper engraving of a branch with apples on it and a vine with leaves along the bottom.

Az unrolled one of the scrolls and saw that it was handwritten in a language he did not understand. "Did you write any of these?"

Nagi shook his head. "My kind does not write their knowledge down. It must be taught by word of mouth and memorized. However, there was once a place in the land of the three kings, where we would travel, and their scribes would write down the world's knowledge so it could never be lost. Even the Druids once had thousands of scrolls in the library. But now it is trapped in a bubble of time, and you must learn to walk through time to visit that place created by a god. The statue one saw when one walked into that library was of the crying god because, as he built it for man, he knew man would one day destroy it."

"A Taoist's knowledge is gained and written down," said Az. "However, it is already known before it is learned. All you have to do is seek it."

"And is that what you are, a Taoist?"

"I am opened-minded," said Az. "That is all I am."

"In my time, whoever was found in possession of the gods' books was exiled here or slaughtered."

Az picked up a book with an apple on the cover, but no branch, and no tree.

"It takes but one piece of knowledge," Nagi said, "to become dangerous."

"What do you mean?"

"Let's say you live in a simple village, and you see a group of lions walking towards the village. You make it back to that village before anyone has even seen the lions. What do you do?"

"Tell the village," said Az.

"Do you tell the whole village or just the people you don't want to be hurt?"

Az thought about that. "Or do I tell no one at all?"

Nagi sat on a high-backed chair in front of the fire.

"Now sit, you must be tired from your journey."

He picked up a long-stemmed pipe that was sitting on the table beside him, then with a long thin stick, he caught a flame from the fire and put it in the candle on the table.

"You are welcome to some if you wish," said Nagi.

Az sat down beside him in the only other chair. Then picked up a small amount of a tar-like substance off a tray on the table. He smelled it, then put it on the end of a wooden stick with a hole on each end. He then put the match-like stick into the fire and lit it. As be breathed it in, he felt like his body was lifted off the ground. His soul became so light it tried to follow the smoke.

"You have opium here," said Az halfway between a question and a statement.

Nagi laughed quietly. "Opium is the gods' golden fruit, either you control it, or it controls you."

–To Dream Again.

Az closed his eyes—no longer able to keep them opened—and as they closed, they were opened again, one outside of his head and the other in.

He was sitting at a table with a group of people, five men he thought, some whose race he could not identify. There was a purple Agotus woman whose race was known as the Agoti in the kitchen.

A human speaks. "I think this is it, the book of Eden. Adam must have stolen it when they forbade him from going back. I have read it! This will change everything. This book holds answers."

The Agotus in the kitchen was cooking what smelled like a stir fry and chopping the meat when a creature—an enormous snake that had the torso of a man with reptilian cobra-like features—slithered through the front door and into the kitchen. Then his tale split off into two legs, and he snapped his finger in front of the purple woman's face.

Az and the rest of the men sitting at the table turned to look at the intruder. They were about to get up just as four black-haired doglike creatures (the Votea) came into the room carrying golden staves and stood around them, the snake's personal guards.

"Sit," said the serpent. "It looks like you were about to eat?"

The dogs stood behind the men and pushed them back down onto their chairs. The woman with the purple skin finished cutting the meat and then began to carve up her own left hand, starting with her fingers and dicing it into pieces as she stared hypnotized by the snake's eyes.

Then Az could smell the meat as she poured the cutting board into the pan. It sizzled as blood squirted everywhere from her stumped wrist. Then the lady grabbed the red-hot pan with her right hand and began to pour it out into the plates on the table, leaving a trail of red blood behind her. Az tried to move, but he couldn't. His stomach began to turn. When she was done serving, she fell to the floor with her eyes opened and did not move.

The snake walked behind one of the men and bit him on the neck injecting his venom into him. The man fell from his chair onto the floor—the snake took the man's place across from Az and began to eat the food on the plate.

"Are you gentlemen not hungry? Well to business then, you are in possession of something that does not belong to you."

The two men sitting to the right of Az began speaking in a different language while the snake just kept staring at Az and eating the food on his plate. He then lifted his right hand into the air pointing his trigger finger to the guards behind to men talking, and in one motion put his finger into the air and tapped it straight down onto the table. The guards pulled out their knives and stabbed the talking men in the back of the neck. Now there was only Az and two men seated to his left.

The man beside the snake said, "It's just a book."

"Did you read the book?" the snake asked.

"Yes." They both replied.

"Then it will be your book forever. Now, are you not going to eat your dinner?"

One of the men looked at the plate of noodles and blue meat.

"That was my wife," he said.

The snake looked at the man seated to Az's right. "And you?"

"I am not worthy to eat in your presence, your worship."

"Then in my presence you will be no more." And again, he lifted his figure up and dropped it onto the table.

The dog behind him stabbed him in the back of the neck, and Az just stared in amazement. The man seated to the snake's left picked up his chopsticks. He ate a noodle from his plate.

"Your kind was one of my best creations," said the snake. "It is too bad the gods could not see it. I will spare your life, and you will live in hell, where you will spend the rest of time with your answers as they become questions and answers again."

The snake turned his lidless gaze on Az.

"Interesting," he said, and with a wave of his scaled hand above the tabletop, Az woke up.

"What the hell!"

"Ah," said Nagi. "You are awake finally. It's lunch, would you like some?"

He handed Az a bowl of soup and noodles. Az looked at it with his stomach still turning, but he was too hungry to refuse and ate it anyways.

When he was done Az said, "I am going to go to my ship today for supplies."

"Just stay close to the treeline and do not turn on any electronical device. There are things in that field that will kill you."

"Thanks for the warning."

Az went back and forth from the crash site for months, burying the bodies and gathering supplies and things he thought would be necessary. Some days he just went in hopes of finding a candy bar still there. Eventually though he forgot about the ship altogether and spent his days hunting or fishing in a small stream they called Styx. It also led to a town in the middle of the forest called Elysium, before joining a raging river on the other side of the forest. The town was a small— one street in an out town—and the buildings were made from stone with shops on the main floor and living quarters upstairs. The paths beside the shops lead to large properties behind them called villas that had huge walls around them and thick wooded doors so that you could not see inside.

A soldier such as Az was given three golden cards when on a planet that does not have proper currency yet. Each card comprised twenty one-gram squares that could be broken from it for trading, and whenever Az buried someone, he took their cards and left them two one-gram squares, one over each eye.

After the first Earth month in hell, Nagi brought Az to Elysium to help carry supplies, and as they walked the five hours along the river into the town, Nagi told him how there is a mighty river on Earth created from the flowing hair of the god Shiva and how Shiva's youngest wife, the goddess Styx, has hair that flows down along her body and into the river Styx.

The town sat on a small hill up from where the river flowed. It had only one cobblestone road that passed through the town. One of the first places in town you saw when you walked up from the river was the bar, and Az was able to trade one gram of gold for two silver obols and six copper leptas, each lepta could buy one large glass of ale, and an obol could purchase a large goatskin container of alcohol (simply called a skin).

The forest seemed to have some kind of enchantment about it that warded off the creatures of the darkness, and Az would see some strange things out of the corner of his eye after one too many drinks. He would swear there were tiny human-like fairies flying around or watching him, but every time he turned to look there was nothing there. The trees in the forest were tall white oaks so thick it would take four men to grasp hands around the trunks.

It was not uncommon, Az knew, for there to be many similarities between neighbouring systems due to asteroid impacts on planets sending plants or seeds and microbes to other planets. When the Earth was only water a planet called Gaia, a smaller planet called Theia, crashed into it, splitting Theia in two. The half that imbedded itself into the earth became known as Pangea, and the other half became known as the moon and moved away from the Earth at two inches a year.

This time in the galaxy was known as the Collision of Life and believed to be how intelligent life in the Milky Way started. The Earth stayed like that for four in a half billion years of years as it was ruled by dinosaurs. Then the second impact came, known as the Collision of War. A giant meteor around 450 metres tall collided directly into the middle of Pangea and dug deep into the Earth, splitting the land mass into continents and creating the Atlantic rift where it collided. That pushed the continents apart at one inch a year. The collision pushed so much material out from Earth it created the Gulf of Mexico and Earth's atmosphere heated up so hot that it boiled the water on Earth turning it into a steamy grave. With the amount of ash and earth stuck in the upper jet streams of the planet, it quickly cooled the Earth as it moved away from the sun and all the steamed water fell to the Earth as snow and became an ice age on earth for over sixty-five million years.

Az had taken the spare room in Nagi's cave and read the books on the shelf with his T2700 and learned to speak several new languages from Nagi who was considered as the old wise Druid priest to the town

When someone first arrived to inhabit their villa, they stopped at Nagi's to speak of how they barely made it past the night creatures or how many of their party was lost. They would offer him a gift at their first arrival, bread, beer, wine, spice, live animals—and on certain nights Nagi would bring the animals to an altar and sacrifice them. The altar stood on a small hill that was surrounded with rocks aligned to the stars along with stone in a spiral pattern all the way up the mound with a stone staircase leading up it. At the top were three stones, two to hold up the altar and one that acted as it. In front of the mound were twelve small altars of dirt surrounded by stones. On each of these, there would be a fire kindled, and each of the twelve leading families would stand around one. Nagi did not believe in wasting a life, and after each of the twelve animals were sacrificed, they would be brought down to one of the fires to be cooked and shared amongst those in attendance. The whole event could last for days by Earth standards, and people would be camped out there or sleeping right on the ground.

At times, Nagi would be called into town to settle disputes. Sometimes, too, he was needed in official state matters during the town meetings. The time that would stand out the most for Az came when four hunting members did not make it back after they had left on a hunt. Nagi was summoned to the town square when one of the bodies was found horribly mutilated from what looked like a creature of the night.

5

We Are All Scared of the Darkness

That night was black, and it rained like a day of war. A man knocked on the door to the cave. When Az opened it he found a pointed eared slender man with a bow standing in the rain under a hooded garment with the shadow of a horse behind him in the dark. Az lead him down the stairs.

"It is a rider from the village with a message, Nagi" Az said.

"My Lord, your presence has been requested at Elysium. It is believed that the killings came from a creature of the night."

"Tell them that I will be there right away."

The man wisped upstairs without another word.

Az went into his room and took out a laser rifle and his sidearm. He thought about putting on his SACS 68, but then he would stand a little too out of place. He slung the rifle over his shoulder and stuck the sidearm into his belt. He then walked outside and stood in the rain, waiting for Nagi to leave the house.

Nagi walked out of the cave, wearing a dark robe with a purple stripe on the sleeve. The only weapon he carried was the wooden staff he used to walk with. Az knew he would give his life to keep that old man safe.

When they reached the town, the street was empty, and the silence was only broken when a flash of red lightning shot down in the distance and the thunder roared. Az had expected a mob with torches and pitchforks. Their guide brought them down one of the paths to a large villa. There was a broad wooden gate in the front that opened when they arrived.

Inside there was a small vineyard and fruit trees along the path to the houses in the back. Az counted four soldiers armed at the door and two with bows standing on top of the wall over the door. The first house looked as though it was for their personal guards. Then there was another wall with a gate, and inside the atrium was a large pool that had three attached houses surrounding it—these three houses comprised a domus. Nagi explained how each of the villas were self-sustaining and many of the crops in them had adapted to need only a small amount of light to keep growing, even in pitch darkness—due to the long darkness when the planet is not facing the sun, the plants stored the energy and sugars in their roots unlike plants on Earth that needed the leaves to absorb the sun and the roots to absorb water. Here most plants stored the sugars and chlorophyll in the roots, and when it stayed dark for too long they slowly sent the needed nourishment with the water back into the rest of the plants. During this time, the leaves on all of the plants turned red instead of green.

As soon as they walked through the second gate, two guards followed their every move. Their guide brought them into the guest quarters in the left domus from the atrium. While it rained, they did nothing but drink, eat, and sleep for two Earth days, and when it stopped raining, they went out to the atrium to meet their hosts and for another day, lay in outdoor beds, eating pork, bread, and grapes while their glasses never emptied of wine.

When Az awoke the day after that, he was brought a white powder, a medicine derived from the one willow tree on the property.

Again, another whole day passed as Az walked out to the atrium for a swim and would just nod at people as they passed. Later he ran into his Magi.

"Tomorrow," said the old man, "we will be going into town to the senate building, one of the guards will bring you when it is time."

"Thank you, Nagi," Az replied.

Az spent the rest of the day in the pool, looking at the dark sky with a billion stars and hundreds of moons projecting enough light to watch the people coming and going from around the pool.

In the morning, a guard came wearing a mix of shiny metal and leather with a Pteruges on [A defensive skirt of leather]. Az picked up his guns, and the soldier asked him if they were weapons, and when he said yes, the soldier told him they would have to stay there if he were to enter the curia. Az placed them on the bed and walked out.

When they reached the curia, the senate had already started. Az saw Nagi sitting to the right but was told to sit to the left. The language of the senate was florid and byzantine, and it seemed to take forever to say anything. Az sat there as he was able to pick up on most of the words, and finally, they came to the business of the missing hunting party. They had suggested sending an entire legion into the forest for it, and Nagi agreed.

However, not only did the town have a druid priest, it also had a witch or seer known as Guanyin who said that if they sent a legion, they would fail. The houses had to submit their best trackers and hunters, two with skilled swordsmen, two archers, and one whose talents ran to knives. The druid also had to go so that he could sacrifice the creature and not disrupt the balance of the forest. Then as Guanyin was about to walk away, she stared into the air as though something were there.

"Wait," said the witch, "there is one more, a foreigner to these lands—*there* he is." And she pointed with her small stick to Az. "Yes, that is him. He must go as well."

As she stared at Az, he stared back into her eerie white eyes as blank as marble orbs. Then the yelling started, and the speaker of the assembly, who sat to the right of Nagi—a man by the name of Malah—stood up and lifted his right hand in the air palm down and moved it from the left side of the room to the right as everyone stopped talking all at once.

Then Malah spoke.

"For thousands of generations, we have been kept safe amongst these trees. It would be wise for us to remember there are forces at work that even the best of us cannot comprehend. If this is how we are to defeat this demon, then so be it."

Each of the twelve houses were given three small pieces of parchment they were to write their best swordsmen, best archer, and best knife master. They were then to place them into the three large vases.

Then Malah clapped his hands, and soldiers came marching bearing the vases and placed them in the middle of the room.

When all of the houses placed their tags into the vases, Malah walked up to the one bearing the names of archers and pulled two names: the Lady Aoibheann from the House of Aoife, and the Lady Ashling from the House of Cliona.

The other houses were outraged and began to yell their protests, claiming it was far too dangerous a mission for women and even going so far as to suggest bad omens for such a decision. These houses, Malah knew, had advanced the names of sons not daughters.

The great man raised his hands and the eyes of the curia fell upon him. "The fates have decided who should go. Who here thinks they are better than the fates?"

The room quieted down as he went to the vase of swords.

"Sir Torii from the house of Mototada, and Sir Balder from the house of Aegir." No one said anything

Then he walked over to the vase of knives. Inside there was but one name, and without reading it everyone knew who should be picked. Lord Al-Amir from the house of Abu.

Malah read the name then bowed his head.

"These five along with the druid priest Nagi and the outlander Az shall form the party of seven who will be our knight walkers and venture out to find the creature. The moon of Plaity will soon cover the moon of Larity, and when that happens, each of the selected houses are to have their hunter ready."

Those assembled nodded their heads and filed out of the building, Az and Nagi among them. In the courtyard, there were handshakes and earnest conversations that carried on back to the bar at familiar tables and rooms.

Az approached the speaker of the assembly who stood with Nagi out front of the curia.

"It seems," Malah said placing his hand on Az's shoulder, "as though your fate was chosen to help us in this time of need."

"It is an honour to be part of the chosen, sir," Az said.

Nagi nodded. "We have much to discuss as to the predictions of the seer, don't we, Malah?"

"Of course, but let's do it over a drink."

While they sat in the bar talking, Az realized that the druid priest and the seer where two sides of one coin that were never to see eye to eye.

When the moons were aligned, Az and Nagi met with the hunters outside of the bar. They all looked so young except for Lord Al-Amir from the house of Abu who was a heavyset man with a bald head and a dark completion. Sir Balder was tall with a strong build and long blond hair and carried a large broadsword and had two axes on his belt. Sir Torii was a short skinny black-haired man who had only one sword with a long double handed handle that hung in a sheath thrust through his sash. Lady Aoibheann had curly red hair to her shoulders with a short bow that barley extruded from the top of her shoulder to just past her left hip and had a quiver of at least thirty arrows. Whereas the Lady Ashling had long brown hair to her waist and carried a longbow that was almost as long as she was tall—in her quiver there were only thirteen arrows.

They walked through the town and stopped at the stables. It was forbidden to bring the horses into town lest the dropping desecrate it.

"Should we bring the horses?" asked Lady Aoibheann.

"How would we track a creature if we cannot see the ground?" replied Lord Al-Amir.

"Well, I am bringing mine anyways," she replied.

The rest of the party did not wait for her and continued out of town. She met up with them at the bridge over the river and jumped off her horse and began walking with it.

At least an Earth week went by while they followed the raging river towards where the body had first been discovered. The archers would compete on who would bring back the best meal, and sometimes Sir Torii would throw his net into the water and pull it out with so many fish they had to throw most of them back. The Lady Ashling had an incredible eye for finding a small blue fruit that grew on the forest floor. They would eat when they woke up, and Sir Balder would take the leftover food from the night before and create a stew with mushrooms and other plants he would gather and cook in a pot he brought with him—one of many pieces of equipment kept with Lady Aoibheann's horse. The two would often scout ahead of the group together, and other members of the party began to suspect a romance brewing judging by the smiles on their faces when they returned.

- The Sacrifice

Finally, they found the remains from one of the missing hunting party or what was left of him anyways.

Lord Al-Amir quickly understood what happened.

"It looks like this is the first spot the creature attacked and the other three tried to fight it. Two of them dumped half their quiver after it first attacked this man and stung him with its poison tail. See the arrows along the tree?"

He pointed in an arch shape pattern of arrows along four of the trees.

"Then here was where the fourth one was standing, and he swung his sword and missed, the blade imbedding into this tree. He must have been wounded by it from this blood, and the three went running that way away from the river as we can see by the broken branches. That was where our little friend went back to this guy to make his kill. From there, this line shows that it went after the wounded one, follow me."

They walked for about twenty minutes into the brush and came across another corpse.

"Here he is, while the other two were shooting arrows at it from over there."

Lord Al-Amir pointed to all the arrows behind him in the trees. Lady Aoibheann pulled the arrows out from the tree, looked at them, and put them in a saddlebag on her horse.

Lady Ashling just stared at her.

"It looks to me," said Lady Aoibheann by way of explanation, "like we are going to need all the arrows we can get for this thing."

Then Lord Al-Amir said, "It looks like the creature is wounded and scared the other two off while it sat here and ate for at least a couple of days. As for the other two, they seem to have been heading for Mount Parnassus to hole up in the old ruins."

"I suspect you are right, Lord Al-Amir," said Nagi. "Let us take the time to set up camp here. Then, after we have rested, we will bury the dead."

After their rest, Lord Al-Amir and Nagi stood by the fire talking while everyone else buried what remained of the two dead. Az, Sir Torii, and Lady Ashling all worked on digging one of the holes together.

"So what is it with Nagi and that mountain?" Az said.

"What do you mean?" asked Lady Ashling

"When Lord Al-Amir said we would be heading towards that mountain, Nagi looked like he had seen a ghost and just stood there staring at it?"

Then Sir Torii looked up at the mountain and back to the two.

"I know why," he said. "That mountain was once home to the great seers. It is said that the fates also lived there when those ruins were once called Phaedriades. Then a great darkness swept over the lands as a race of giants roamed through the lands, killing everyone, and destroying all other gods and their shrines. It is the origin of the twelve houses and something Lady Ashling would know if she paid more attention to history."

Lady Ashling shot Sir Torii a skeptical look. "They are just kids' stories to scare us, nothing more."

"So what happened next?" Az asked.

"The mainland is separated by twelve different realms, and each realm with its own king, there each realm is separated twelve times again. It is said that Nagi himself came to each of the kings of the twelve realms to unite them and kill off the race of giants, and as a reward, each of the twelve kings were allowed a small property inside of Elysium. Not only did they defeat the giants in battle. They hunted the rest down until there were none left."

Lady Ashling laughed. "There are no giants and there never has been."

Sir Torii looked at Lady Ashling with anger. "Your age can quickly be seen in your actions, for your fire burns brightly still, and you are quick to dismiss what you do not know."

"So why is it that Nagi does not want to go up there?" Az asked again.

"Because by the time Nagi had gathered the armies, the giants had already destroyed the temple Phaedriades and burned much of this forest."

Az stood there staring at the mountain in the distance while the other two piled a cairn of rocks over the grave. When they finished, they went and helped Lady Aoibheann and Sir Balder and once the body was buried Lady Aoibheann spoke out loud,

"The body now rests in the ground
The soul is free to roam around
Until the day he is born again
Into a new body into a new friend"

They all nodded their heads and went back to camp for what could have been rabbit for all Az knew. Lord Al-Amir had killed and skinned it with one of his knives.

When Lord Al-Amir said they would travel after their next rest. They all knew, he knew, the other two were already dead.

Everyone slept early except Lord Al-Amir and Az who were sitting by the fire. Then Lord Al-Amir took out one of his knives and placed it on his figure so it sat perfectly still.

"A perfect knife comes from a perfect craftsman of not just metal but wood. You see the weight of the blade is equal to the weight of its handle so that, when it is thrown, it will stay perfectly straight with the amount of force you use to throw it. But do not mistake force for muscle my young friend. If you try using all your strength to throw it, the steel will take the strength and veer off course. No, you must understand that the blade, even when it is no longer in your hand, it is still part of your arm, and when you release it, your hand will move the knife as it cuts through the element of air."

Then with the grace of a dancer, he threw the blade, as it missed the first tree and stuck into a snakes by its head to the trunk of a tree slightly to the right it had been slithering down.

"Could you retrieve my knife for me, my young friend?"

"Yes, Lord Al-Amir," Az replied and brought back both the knife and the snake that was as long as Az was tall.

Lord Al-Amir skinned and gutted the snake into the fire. He then wrapped its flesh around a large stick and cooked it on the fire for Az and him to eat.

For three more days, they walked to the base of the mountain, and Az was able to start picking up the creature's tracks. The only thing he knew about it was that it had hundreds of little legs that left a line wherever it walked, and the only reason he was able to pick up on it was the green bloodstains he was noticing it left.

It was Lady Ashling who saw it first.

"There it is." Both she and Lady Aoibheann had arrows nocked in an instant. But Az could see nothing but darkness along the outline of the hill.

"It's moving up the mountain," said Sir Balder. "Too far to reach, we are going to have to climb after it."

"No," said Lord Al-Amir. "That is exactly what it wants us to do and why it stayed here, waiting for us to close in on it. The other two must have used this as a defensive position, and from these boulders it looks like they were trying to keep it from climbing the mountain.

"I agree with Lord Al-Amir," Nagi said. "There is a gentler slope with a path not too far from here, we will take that."

Sir Balder led the horse by the reigns while the Lady Aoibheann's eyes never left the hillside an arrow held nocked in her bow across her lap.

At first Az did not understand why, but Lady Ashling walked behind him and kept her bow in her right hand and held on to Az's shirt with her left. It was so she could stay watching the mountainside while Az led her forward.

"Rock," Lady Aoibheann yelled.

And they all looked up and were able to step out of the way so it landed between them. This happened eight more times, and the men became used to looking back down after the rock hit the ground.

That was until the eighth time

The eighth time the creature was there and had used the rock as a distraction. It was close enough they could have touched it. Lady Aoibheann shot off ten arrows as it scurried up the hill, and Lady Ashling shot twice, once just under it when she first saw it, stopping it from being able to go any further down the hill and another that clipped it as it pulled the arrow out from its wing. The simplest description of it would be a manta ray seven feet wide, five feet long and fast. With the dark rocks, it looked like a shadow cast on them not something alive and moving. Az got two shots off at it with his sidearm and missed both times.

"It's hurt and slow," said Lady Aoibheann who was standing on her stirrups and threw Lady Ashling's arrow down to her.

"We are almost at the path. That is why it took this chance to attack," replied Nagi.

Az put his sidearm into his belt so that he could hold his rifle aiming it up the mountain and could not see anything but rock through its scope despite the sophisticated infrared settings it boasted.

When they reached the path, Lady Aoibheann dismounted and slapped her horse's flank, sending it running off into the woods.

While they ascended upwards, Lord Al-Amir stayed dangerously close to the edge, looking down occasionally even while some stones under him gave way and fell, but he never lost his footing.

They reached a circular stone structure only around four feet tall with some larger pillars still erect. The rest of it had been destroyed. The last two bodies lay inside the circle with nothing but a smell to know they were once alive.

Lady Aoibheann picked up an arrow and put it in her quiver, and that was where Az realized they had the same markings as hers did. Az could hear it scurrying first to his right then his left and knew the echoes were playing with his mind. Then a second later, twenty feet above them, it began to glide down. Both the archers emptied their quivers, and Az unloaded his rifle and began to shoot at the creature's head with his sidearm—it veered from them to the left. A second later it climbed up one of the pillars towards them, and when it jumped, it froze there in mid-leap. The ruins had turned green with the glow of the rocks as Nagi held his glowing staff aloft. Then Sir Torii stabbed in between the hundreds of legs that looked as though they could stab into him. Sir Balder first cut off its tail and then its head.

When Nagi's staff touched the ground, everything went dark again, and the creature fell to the ground. Lord Al-Amir walked up to it and pulled eighteen knives out from its right wing and two more from just under its mouth. The archers retrieved whatever arrows they could from the corpse.

"Bring wood," said Nagi, "so we can burn its foul remains."

Nagi pulled a small blade out from under his robe and began to carve symbols on the creature's skin. The rest of them gathered wood with Lord Al-Amir and Sir Balder seeming to compete to see who could haul the most wood at one time. When they finished there stood a six-foot-high funeral pyre, and they put the remains of the creature upon it. Then they buried the dead.

When they were done, Nagi waved his right hand over the pile of wood as a small flame lit from the bottom to the top.

Lady Aoibheann put two fingers in her mouth and whistled. Moments later her horse came running up the hill. Then from her sack she pulled out a skin for everyone to drink and produced a flute that she played while they danced around the fire drinking.

Then Lady Aoibheann and Sir Torii disappeared into the darkness.

Lady Ashling took Az by the hand and lead him onto the grass outside the ruins. As she began to lay down on her back Az followed her eyes, hypnotized by the night.

"Are you a pagan?" she asked.

"Darling, I am tonight."

When they woke after the drink, the sun began to show from behind the moon, and the twenty years of night had finally been lifted. Az looked out over the forest at all the red leaves, and as they walked home, the red leaves fell to the ground in slow graceful spirals as green leaves began to take their places and flowers began to show. Again, Az could see the pixies flying around along with birds and butterflies and other beautiful coloured creatures he had never seen before.

When they entered the town, it was already engaged in celebration for the festival of the sun, and after the next rest, they were brought into the senate. Lady Aoibheann and Lady Ashling wore beautiful white clothing and had their hair braided back. Sir Balder, Sir Torii, and Lord Al-Amir wore the rich traditional garb of their houses. They were made to stand in the middle of the senate as the speaker of the house, Malah, placed crowns of mistletoe upon their heads. And for three more Earth days, they celebrated. Az slipped away on the third day and began to follow the river back when he walked right into Lady Ashling who was sitting by the river whistling to three small bird that flitted from nearby branches.

"It seems it is your time to go," she said.

"I have a mission that I have already been too long away from."

"Your mission will only lead you to loneliness and death."

"Perhaps," said Az. "But if I don't complete it, then someone else will have to."

"As a soldier you are slipping from the fight," said Lady Ashling.

She stood up and walked over to him, with the sun's rays and mist shining behind her as she stood staring in his eyes. Then she kissed him on the cheek.

"Safe travels my friend." And with that she walked past him and back towards the town.

–The Highway

Az walked into Nagi's cave to see him sitting in his chair watching the fire dance.

"It seems to be my time to leave," said Az.

"I must go into the city for some business as well," said Nagi. "We will leave after the next rest. That will give you enough time to gather the things you will need to complete your mission."

Az thought about his mission and how it felt like so long ago since he was brought there. His eyes felt different, like his perception of reality was fading. But then, it could have also been from finally seeing sunlight again. He walked to the clearing where the ship had crashed and looked at how the vegetation had overtaken it, and the new trees were already taller than the ship.

He sat in the pilot's chair and stared out the broken front window. A thin crescent of brilliant sun was just beginning to emerge from behind the large moon that had shielded it.

He then walked around the wreckage and looked at the foot soldier outfits he had piled along one of the ship's walls. Then felt the connection scar on his stomach that had healed. This once had connected him to the food and waste management system of his suit. But no longer.

There was nothing left for him there. He had become dependent on the scenery. A common thing for soldiers. Eye-lag they call it. The inability to move from one's surroundings for fear that the next place will be even worse.

He returned to the cave, and in his room, he looked at all the things he collected, thinking he would need them when he left. Then he went out to the fireplace and sat in his chair. From the large bowl of tar on the table, he picked up and smoothed a small ball. He placed it on the end of the pipe and smoked it.

Again, his eyes open as they shut.

He was in front of a large lake of liquid crystal without so much as a ripple in sight. Floating over the water was another purple Agotus with silk purple garments. There was a sound in the wind, like women singing, but her humming would not let them show themselves. Az felt like he was floating with each step he took toward her—his mind had no other thoughts but to get to her.

The closer he got, the more it felt like something was pulling him back. He tried to reach her as he lost his breath from whatever was pulling him away, and he collapsed just before reaching her unable to breathe, and his eyes closed to open again.

He awoke to find himself in his bed and looked around at the room again. Then he went over to his armoire, and the only things he grabbed were his sidearm, a field knife, and his T2700. He reached under the bed and grabbed the briefcase, then he walked out to the living room where Nagi was sitting in his chair staring at the fire.

"Are you ready?" asked the old man.

"It is time."

Nagi waved his hand over the fire, and all that was left was a puff of smoke that travelled up the chimney. Then Az went to the lanterns on the wall, ran his finger in the air from the top down, as the flames followed his fingers and went out.

They walked up the stairs, and Nagi put some logs in front of the door. If you lock the door, people will think there is something inside worth stealing. If instead you only put something in front of the door, then if someone comes by, they will know you are not home.

They walked down a winding path and out from the treeline. Then they made their way down the grassy hillside onto a dirt road and again walked another four Earth hours until they reached a broad stone road that cut through the hills. It looked as though it went on forever, full of people going nowhere.

All forms of life in the entire universe seemed to be on that highway as though hell was once a cosmic crossroads that had become cut off from the rest of the galaxy. Or perhaps it was a prison once, so vast and remote, and with so many different languages that most people would never be bothered to learn another language (although everyone in Elysium communicated in ancient Greek regardless of their native tongue). Az watched everyone coming and going, fascinated by all the different humanoid species there were. Some travelled by buggy pulled by creatures—some creatures rode other creatures. It was a scene hard to describe to someone who hadn't seen it, not without using what one already knows, and what one already knows would not paint a picture of what one does not know. They all were *walking* on that stone road, however; there were no motorized vehicles of any kind. The road itself was a feat of remarkable engineering, each stone, though utterly irregular, interlocking with the next no matter what shape they were as if they were placed down then melted together, and along the sides were ditches for water runoff.

"Who built roads like this?" Az asked.

"No one knows, it is said they were built by a race of giants long ago."

Nagi and Az passed like two blood cells that had flowed into a main artery. They would occasionally sleep at the side of the highway in the treeline and bathe in a river when they came to one and fill up their skins with water. They would also fish in the river and try their luck at a little hunting. Sometimes they stopped in some of the small hamlets for a night our two for rest and drink.

There were no cities or towns on the main highway, and when Az asked why, Nagi smiled as though the answer were obvious.

"It is because that would be the place everyone would attack, after all, the road would lead right to it."

On their journey, Nagi wore a long white robe with a purple strip along the hood and on the cuffs of the sleeves.

One day, Nagi just stopped and stood in the middle of the highway without any explanation. Az had kept walking for a few minutes before turning around and noticing him there. Az turned and walked back to his travelling companion.

"Why did you stop?"

"I am waiting for someone."

Around twenty minutes later Az asked, "How do you know you are waiting for someone?"

"Because there he is," Nagi said, and a man wearing the same robe (but with a red striping) walked up to him.

"Have you seen Zan?" Nagi asked the man.

"No, but I am sure you will," the other replied.

Nagi nodded his head and continued walking again for what seemed like forever.

When they came to a fork in the road, they took the right path, and Az could finally see the blue of the ocean in the distance and feel the cool breeze that blew off of it. Or perhaps it was just the sky and his eyes were playing tricks on him.

A few earth weeks later, they took rest at a large inn that looked like a castle. It had two grand doors, and on either side of the curved entrance a very large dogman stood guard. These guards looked kind of like the ones in Az's dream— except that the ones in the dream were black with short hair and a lot smaller than these brown long-haired dogs who had to be standing ten feet tall at least. They were wearing brown leather kilts created of small leather pads stitched together. Around their necks were hung huge medallions of gold. In their right hand was a gold staff, and a sheathed sword (that on them looked like a knife) hanging from the belt.

As Az walked past them, he turned and looked at Nagi.

"Why the armed guards at the door?"

"The Votea, you mean? This is a big planet that is always at war with itself."

Inside the grand doors was a large courtyard with a market selling trinkets and food. Along the walls were rooms and apartments that, by Az's count, were stacked seven stories towards the sky. Nagi and Az stopped at one of the market restaurants and sat down at the table. Nagi ordered meat that looked like one of the things walking on the highway being rotisserie cooked over hot coals.

While they sat there eating, Nagi ordered them flat warm ale served in clay cups. After the first sip that hit Az's lips, he put down the half empty glass looked at Nagi and said "Such a missed state of mind my friend."

They didn't move from their chairs for hours except to go to the washroom. Eventually one of the orbiting moons covered the sun overhead and night came crawling amongst them. At that point, a body fell from an upper balcony down and landed by Az, splattering blood across his face. He paid a coin to a boy walking around with rolled wet towels and wiped his face and threw it on the body as it was dragged away.

Nagi placed three silver bits on the table. "My evening has come to an end. That will cover the rest of your night, and when you feel like you have had your fill of both food and drink, give this coin to the man on the stairs, and he will escort you to your room.

Then he handed over a larger bronze coin that Az put in his pocket.

Az and the waitress had a routine down. He would put his empty pottery cup upside down on the table, and she would bring him another ale. He would hand her a silver obol, and she would give him back eight bronze coins and eleven copper leptas and one made of nickel. Then he could give her the nickel for another beer. And when he gave her a copper lepta, she gave back one nickel. At one point in the night, a man who had two women with him sat at his table, and Az was able to practice some of one of the languages he learned well at the cave.

Deep into the night, Az excused himself and walked to the stairs. He handed the short round man the bronze coin, and the man had a really cute blue woman walk him up the stairs as he followed her while she lit the way with a small candle inside of a glass.

Az pondered the next action that was to be taken as they climbed to the fourth floor and the woman opened the door and escorted him inside. She then used her candle to light the one that sat on the only small table beside the bed and Az could see there was only that table, a bed and a small brass bathtub in it. She pointed to the tub, and Az nodded. She then put out her hand, and Az handed her a copper coin. She then left and a few minutes later the warm steamy water started to flow into the tub.

He heard a knock at the door and another lady was standing there with a tray. He had no idea what she was saying, but she had a bunch of bottles on the tray and a number of small folded pieces of paper. She picked up a bottle and pointed to the tub, and Az nodded. Then she opened one of the small pieces of paper and held it up to Az's nose. He nodded, and she handed it to him. He gave her one of his silver coins, and she handed him a pipe and a stick and another small bottle of some kind of strong alcohol that she motioned he could drink. He closed the door and locked it with a large cast iron bolt then left his clothes in a pile on the floor over the small briefcase and sat in the tub.

When he was done, he laid in the bed and leaned over to the end table. He inhaled the smoke while sitting on the bed with his back against the wall. He took one last long draw on the pipe as the darkness was now forming in his soul as he fell asleep.

Az woke to a tap at the door and wondered how long he had been out for. He opened the door—which he could see by way of the small amount of light coming in around it—and a blue-skinned woman brought in breakfast on a tray and placed it on the little table. Az tipped her a nickel, and she left.

When he was done eating, she took the food tray and put it onto the balcony as he went down the stairs and found Nagi sitting at a table with another man who was wearing a leather hat. He looked to be some kind of a hunter or trapper.

"Did you have a good sleep?" Nagi asked when Az approached.

"It was okay."

Nagi introduced the man he was sitting with as Kln. The man stood and tipped his hat to Az. Nagi stood up shook the man's hand. When Kln left, Nagi sat back down and gestured to a seat.

"Please join me."

Az sat down and began to pick at the fruit on the table. They drank the black coffee—there were two things that beat Az to any planet he had ever visited (at least any planet that hosted humans): coffee and opium. He was always a cream and sugar man himself, but here there was nothing but black with coffee grinds in the bottom. He finished his breakfast without saying a word.

When they walked out of the inn, Nagi turned to him.

"Almost there."

Az looked at the ocean in front of them. It was massive, and he could see some small sailing vessels in the distance.

6

Between Hell and High Water

When they finally reached the cliff's edge, Az realized that the whole time he thought he was walking towards the water he'd been mistaken. This was not where the ocean met the land. He looked at the huge city below, a stone metropolis with a huge stone wall around it with castles and pyramids as though the metropolis was many small cities that merged together over time and stretched too far for the eye to see the end. Along the docks he could see massive sailing ships, and the breeze was crisp and cool.

"Welcome to Annwn," said Nagi. "It was once seven smaller cities that battled for control of the ports here. Until the population became too overwhelming. Now each of the seven control a gate into Annwn. This is the only place where the cliffs do not drop directly into the ocean and the most direct sea route to the islands of the spices."

"It is like a work of art," Az replied.

Nagi only snickered. "We will take the cart down into Jahannam, one of the cities."

The cart looked just as phenomenal as the city. It had amazing artwork carved into the design of the wood paneling on it. Beautiful women with their breasts showing and people making love. It reminded him of what pictures of hell looked like in the sixteenth century on Earth. There were two carts and a pulley system—it would have been called a funicular back on Earth. While one cart was at the top, one was at the bottom of the hill. The carts ran on steel tracks and were pulled by a huge steel cable and at the top of the hill there was a circled gear the wire would ride on. As far as Az could see, the carts acted as each other's counterweights, making them easier to lower and raise.

As they approached the cart to enter, they were met again by three of the gigantic Votea who stood at the entrance. They were enormous—they had to be fifteen feet tall at least and seemed to be the guardians of Annwn.

"It is said that their kind once ruled the Earth as mighty giants for the gods," said Nagi. "When the gods decided that man, as a species, was too uncontrollable and unpredictable, they caused the Earth to be covered in a mighty flood erasing man from the universe—except for all humans who weren't sent here that is."

"And yet the Earth is still ours, and the gods are nowhere to be seen."

Nagi shook his head. "The fates decide not the gods."

"So the fates control the gods?"

"God is a name given to those who have power by those who do not understand the power yet. Those who can control the universe, control the gods."

"Then who can control those who control the universe?"

"Ahh," said Nagi. "They must govern each other, they are older than time itself."

"The time before time?"

"Correct. It is good that you know of that."

"Do they also control the fates?" asked Az.

"No," said Nagi. "The fates are a different entity altogether. When a new form of life is born, so are their fates, and if that new form of life is extinguished, then their fates to will die with them."

"So you believe we have no control over our destinies, Nagi?"

"I did not say that, did I? Your plan was to never set foot on this mainland, and yet here you are. Everyone on your ship is dead except for the person who sat exactly where you did. You are also a soldier, so how many times has the person beside you been killed and not you? You seem to have a habit of tempting the fates, and yet here you are. How would you explain that?"

"Before I met you, I would have just called it luck."

Az walked past the guards, staring at the one on his right as it looked down at him unmoving. The creature growled when Az met its gaze and walked onto the trolley. As he looked out the window of the lift side, he could see people farming with animals and plows.

"Why don't they simply use powered machines to farm? Would it not be more efficient?"

"And what would the people do if the machines did all their work? One machine instead of fifty thousand people maybe more," Nagi said. "And the animals, what would they do?"

"Be released back into the wild."

Nagi looked at him. "There is no wild on a planet. A planet must be created, controlled, and shaped. Even a planet with no life on it but vegetation will destroy itself, overgrowing and choking itself out. You see we are the blood, and every planet we are on, we become part of its blood, sometimes like a disease, sometimes like the cure."

"And what is it that they are farming there?"

"The only things needed to feed a city—hops, barley, wheat, corn, and grain. Everything else is grown farther out or is brought here on those ships."

Az stared out the window again and watched as the people in the fields became closer and closer like ants under a magnifying glass. He was in awe at the beauty and majesty of the city. He pointed at one huge round building with no top and another building in an egg shape with a round roof on one end.

"Is that a coliseum and that an amphitheatre?"

"After the next rest we will go see a show, if you want to, of course?" asked Nagi as he starred out the window at the city below.

"Yes, I think I would like that."

When the cart came to a complete stop, they exited into a street market where it looked like merchants were selling, well, everything. Az stopped at a vendor with women and men staked on stage and their arms tied above their heads.

"There are slaves here?" he asked.

"Slavery and war are a form of population control. Just be glad you are on this side of that stage. Because they are also considered as food here."

Nagi looked into Az's face and smiled.

"Well come on, do you want to trade that damn case of gold you have been lugging around into viable money? Besides, if they catch you trying to trade with unmarked currency here, you will be on that stage."

Nagi and Az walked to a large pyramid with stairs running up the middle and huge pillars on both sides of each step. They stopped at the bottom and stared at the staircase to the sky.

"What happens if you can't make it up the stairs?"

"If you cannot afford to have someone do it for you," Nagi said, "then you have no business trading with the Kamikiri."

Inside the pyramid, the Kamikiri looked like a man-size termite behind the counter, and when they got to it, Nagi nodded his head at Az, and Az opened the briefcase to reveal gold and silver bars about half an inch thick. The Kamikiri took the bars and returned with a book with scratches on it, some squiggly lines and dots. Nagi squiggled something in it then told Az to sign in one corner.

"This is the first page of your book," said Nagi.

The Kamikiri then said something to Nagi, and Nagi looked at Az.

"He wants to know if you want to open an account, or do you just want some carrying bags? The accounts are transferable in all cities worldwide."

"I will open an account and take three of those lines and two of those dots."

"A fair amount of cash to carry," Nagi said. "Each line is a hundred gold coins and dots are fifty of silver. Seeing as the rate of gold and silver is always changing, they store the amount separately for a service charge, of course."

Nagi and the Kamikiri spoke back and forth until he looked at Az again.

"Would you like to have anyone added to the account, Az?"

"While if I do not make it back, Nagi, I guess that would be you."

"Very well." Nagi turned and talked back and forth with the Kamikiri.

"Well," Nagi said, "write in the amount you want to withdraw over in that red section."

A bag for each marking was placed on the table, and Az put them in his Mickey pocket and transferred his flask to his back pocket.

When Nagi made a request, they rolled out a bookshelf with huge books, and one was opened on the table. Nagi then talked business with the teller as Az sat there wondering what he was talking about as he tried to find the language on his T2700.

Finally, after what seemed like an entire day, the termite brought some small bags of money and put them on the table. Nagi picked them up and felt them like a doctor that just told someone to turn and cough, then clipped them to the inside of his robe as they left back into the heat and sun.

They walked a few blocks down and went into a store where a grasshopper, you could say, was tending the counter. Nagi handed him a few coins, and the shopkeeper scraped some black tar out of a jar and wrapped it with what looked a kind of like waxed butcher paper. Then he handed a few cigars with it—or at least that's what they looked like. Nagi pointed a finger at one of the large boxes on the counter, and the grasshopper clicked it twice and two wooden tablets that looked like dominos come out of the front. Nagi looked at the design of the dots and lines on the domino piece and rolled it along the pictures on the box. With no matches, he handed them back to the grasshopper, and they were put back into the top of the box.

Hoping they were going to be fine cigars, Az put some coins on the counter then pointed to the tar and cigars. The grasshopper handed them over, and Az made a fist then put out his thumb and pinkie finger and tapped at a box. It was a universal sign to symbolize six.

Az then matched two of the dominos pieces with the pictures on the box. One of them dots, the other angled lines. He handed back the losers first then showed the clerk the winners, and the clerk handed Az back his coins and added some bronze coins with it. Az thought of his night at the inn and smiled then handed Nagi one of the bronze coins and three silver coins back.

"I see you are not as new to the world as I thought," said Nagi.

Az clapped him on the shoulder. "Well what do you say we get ourselves a drink?"

"Remember when shopping, always shop modestly," said Nagi. "It is a reward in itself."

"Sure," said Az, "and beer is always a great reward."

Nagi led them to a bar, and they sat down at a table where, to Az's surprised, there was a cute human waitress wiping off their table with a cloth that had a red tinge to it.

The only thing better than the beer here is the view!

As the afternoon glow flowed into the night, they smoked their wonderful cigars and drank the warm flat ale. Nagi ordered some food, and someone in white came and pulled the middle of the table off revealing that there was a pot under it. Water was added, and a bowl of oil was put under it and lit on fire. Then a cart was brought to them with small ocean creatures and herbs.

First Nagi put some of the spices and green herbs into the pot. Then they sat there for an hour or two dunking odd-looking creatures and rolls of meats into the water to cook. At one point, Nagi put a hard noodle roll on the strainer and sat it in the water.

Aha, thought Az, *that's what these things are for*—and he did the same. After the noodles softened, they put them into a small bowl where they added some of the now broth-like water in it as well and added some herbs.

When they'd had their fill of eating and drink, Az left a gold coin on the table, and Nagi took them a few doors down where they walked in the front door of a building with no windows. At the counter, the man behind it gave them both bracelets with scratches on them, and they walked through the door to another counter where the man looked at the scratches on the bracelets and handed them baskets with towels in it. Nagi took off his clothes and placed them in the box while Az followed suit. Then they grabbed their towels and walked through the next door.

"How do you know everything won't get stolen in these places?" asked Az

"That is why we go to bathhouses and not whorehouses."

The next room featured a huge pool and what looked like a steaming hot tub running into it. The room was covered in blue marble and had pillars throughout it. Az dropped his towel on the floor and dove into the pool.

"I wish I had money to tip them, said Az, "but it's in the basket."

"All payments are made at the end of your stay."

After some time of just floating around, Nagi walked out of the pool and dried off, and so did Az, curious to see what to do next.

They walked through another door where another man handed them silk shorts and a robe from behind a desk. They put them on and walked up the stairs beside the desk to another desk where a lady escorted Az to a room. As he walked away, Nagi spoke up.

"I will wake you in the morning."

Az awoke when Nagi knocked on the door and walked in with two black coffees.

"Pleasant night?"

"I have had worst," said Az.

After that, they headed off to the market where on the way a man with a white robe and a purple stripe stopped to talk with Nagi introducing himself as Zan.

"We have much to discuss," Nagi said.

They walked with their hoods up looking at the ground muttering something that Az could not understand. When they reached a gated wall, they bowed their heads to each other and Zan walked away.

—Down the Rabbit Hole We Go

They had reached the edge of Jahannam and the gate of Ladha, and again the Votea stood guard. This time there was a centaur as well. Nagi took out a scroll and showed it to the centaur. As he explained to Az that you had to have a pass to be able to cross between one realm and the other.

As soon as they walked through the gate the breeze from the ocean stopped.

"Why is it so hot here?" asked Az.

"This part of the city is cut off from the ocean by the Realm of Saqar. We must walk through Ladha to get there."

Az looked around at the people of Ladha—they had green scaly skin and the whites of their eyes were yellow, but they otherwise looked human. Nagi had a way of taking the long way everywhere, except here. Az could feel the heels of his feet cracking from the heat of the road, through his boots by the time the next gate was in site.

At the gate into Saqar, there was a thick wall and this time the Votea and the centaur stood in the arch between the realms so the breeze would hit them. Again, Nagi showed his pass, and they walked into Saqar.

The first thing beyond the gate was a giant fountain of Poseidon with his trident. They rinsed their heads in the cold water. Then sat for a time at a small shop in the square where they served a cooled fruit juice of some kind.

From there they walked only a few more hours into a cool wind that came off from the water until stopping at a corner with a shop on one side that also took up the corner and a Butcher shop on the other. In between was an iron gate that Nagi unlocked and walked through. Nested behind them was a courtyard with a dried pond that had a brass fountain of a small-breasted woman with two fauns, one on either side of her. Az found it interesting how similar the fauns looked so much like the medieval depictions of the devil.

Around the courtyard stood overgrown trees choked with vines, and behind that a three-storey brick building. Az and Nagi walked through the courtyard, and as they walked, it was as though the trees shrank in his presence embarrassed by the way they let themselves grow, as the vines disappeared back into the ground and large fruit that looked like peaches hung from the branches. He then touched the brass sculpture of the woman on the shoulder as though she were a long-lost lover and water appeared from nowhere and ran down her long hair as it began to fill the pond, and lotus flowers grew out of nowhere in the water and bloomed.

He walked into the stone house and the candles flickered to life of their own accord.

"I am tired from our journey and need to rest. My quarters are on the third floor. You will find three guest rooms on the second floor. You are welcome to your choice of room."

"Thank you, Nagi."

"After our dreams have passed, we will go to the docks and find you a boat."

Az turned to thank the old man, but he had vanished like dust on the wind. He walked to the back of the large opened room and found a staircase to the second floor. He took the first room he found and lay on a large canopy bed. The pillows and blankets felt so soft and cool he fell asleep almost instantaneously.

The last thing he remembered before he awoke was hearing screaming and the sound of panicked footfalls running down a hallway of stone. He could not see anyone but heard a voice begging for help. Then he awoke.

He walked downstairs to find Nagi, wearing a white toga with purple striping and a purple *sagum* [a cloak fastened over one shoulder]. Az still had his brown pants and shirt on with a vest that he switched out with his spare set of clothes. They walked out to the courtyard, and Nagi picked a fruit from one of his trees and offered it to Az who shook his head—he could not find his hunger.

When they had arrived, Az hadn't seen a soul on the streets in this realm, now however, the streets were packed. There were hundreds of humans. The guards had on shiny armour and leather with a red sagum, and the nobility were wearing white togas with red striping. The rest of the people looked as though they had light sheets of different colours wrapped around them.

They walked to the ocean and down a hundred-step stone staircase cut into the wall. At the bottom, they walked onto the wooden docks while cargo boxes and animals were being carried or pulled on carts by donkey-like creatures. They walked to a large wooden desk where sat the port master; two human guards stood behind him.

Az could pick up on the conversation that Nagi was having with him, and the port master said that the next free ship could be at least fifty moons away. Az put a stack of ten silver obols onto the table. When the man leaned forward to pull the coins back, Az noticed he was missing his legs.

The port master said, "A fleet of ships just returned to Hutamah with their cargo stolen by pirates and in desperate need of repairs, lest they end up at the bottom of the harbour. If you want a free ship, it will be quicker to pay for the repairs on one of those then to wait for one here."

Nagi nodded, and they walked off.

When they walked to the gates Nagi did not have the papers to pass through to the next realm and asked to speak with the office. A centaur road off and returned before the next moon had even cast its shadow, handing Nagi a paper rolled with a seal. He looked at Az as be broke the seal and unrolled the scroll. A small grin crept across his features as he read.

> *The Queen Demeter requests your presence*
> *at her palace in the Realm of Hutamah.*
> *If you choose to enter our realm,*
> *Mlakalies, the presenter of this scroll,*
> *will be your guide.*

Az nodded, and Nagi handed the scroll back to Mlakalies. And they walked on either side of the centaur as they passed through the gate. As they entered Hutamah, Az realized why, even from above, each realm's construction looked so different. It was a matter of resources and building materials available to the different realms. On such a large planet, to pass through these seven gates could span more distance than all of Earth and Venus combined. Here there was so much sand that the buildings themselves looked to be built of sandstone unlike the hard, quarried stone buildings and cobblestone roads he had already passed through.

They journeyed to a river that cut through the land and emptied into the mighty ocean. To the people of this place, the river was life, and the further you walked from the river the closer to death you were.

They walked past many pyramids in the distance that looked like mountains, and when they came to the palace it was a grand two-storey pillared building that backed onto jagged mountains that seemed poised to protect its flank. They walked up the stairs to a huge opened area—large enough, Az thought, to land one of their spaceships on. However, there was no one to greet them. They walked across the hot empty stones and into another large chamber, and Az knew this was not a sanctioned meeting.

Finally, they entered a room that had a whole smorgasbord of food laid out on it, and at the end was young Queen Demeter. Her back turned to them as she stared out the window.

Mlakalies stamped his hoof on the ground as she turned. He bowed low.

"May I present to you his grace the Druid Master Nagi and his apprentice Azuse."

The queen nodded her head and Mlakalies was dismissed. She walked up to them.

"I was only a child the last time you came here, your grace." She kissed the ring on his left hand.

"You summoned me, and I came." Nagi replied.

"And for that I am grateful," she said, "for there is a matter that only you can help me with. My daughter Persephone has been kidnapped by the warlord Hades, and my husband will not send troops into Sa'eer for fear that, if he does, the tribes will unite and attack our realm."

She walked over to a painted statue depicting a young woman with pale skin, red hair, and a blue dress as she ran her right hand along its cheek.

"As you can see, Persephone is quite beautiful and does not belong with those savage barbarians."

When Nagi looked at her, Az could see the empathy in his eyes.

"As you know," he said. "I am banished from these lands and have been for quite some time. For me to enter into Sa'eer would cause a war far greater than the one your husband worries about."

Then he looked at Az and back to her.

"However, my young apprentice, here, is new to this world and is in need of a ship to Origon. Since your docks seem to have the only available fleet, I would imagine, once repaired, you would have no problem to charter one for him?"

"Of course not, if you return with my daughter, he will be rewarded with passage on three of the fastest ships of my personal fleet."

They both turned to look at Az.

He looked at them both as though this had been planned—or perhaps fated—long before he had ever met them.

"Let's begin, then, shall we?"

—Sa'eer

Nagi and Az were escorted to the gates of Sa'eer by six of the queen's personal guards. It was not until Az could see the ballistae mounted atop the wall facing into it that Nagi explained.

"Sa'eer also has no access to the ocean as it is a place of exile. It does have a labyrinth of caves that can lead to the top of the cliffs. But you must stay out of there, for not only is it unheard of to navigate through, it is also guarded by minotaurs that will kill any human on site. The cliff's shadow is forever cast onto this land, making it forever cold. The first city you enter through these gates is called the city of Mnemosyne. There you will find the River of Sorrows that is fed from a natural spring that flows out of Hades, palace called Erebus. You must pay a silver obol for a ride on one of their charons. They are small river boats that will take you upstream. Do not put your hand in the water, for there are creatures in there that will eat you to your bone. Once inside the gates of Erebus, you will find her in a small room looking down upon the river."

"How do you know that, Nagi?"

"I can see it," he replied.

When they reached the gate, there were three Votea standing guard, and one of the queen's men handed one of them a scroll. They removed the squared wood logs that had been wedged into the ground to hold the giant doors closed, and as they pulled them opened, the hinges gave off a loud screech as though it was in pain. Then they lifted the huge iron portcullis from inside a small room above. Nagi just smiled at him as Az walked through into the room with two of the Votea and the portcullis closed behind them while the one in front of him began to open. While waiting, Az looked up when he smelled hot tar and saw the holes in the floor above. Then the two Votea opened the large wooden door and closed it behind Az.

He walked out into a large courtyard of dirt with some small shrubs growing and stone buildings around it. Nagi was right, it was a lot colder there, and his head quickly turned to something that moved in the shadow. His hand quickly grasped his sidearm. He looked at a small alley between two buildings that would take him out from the open and timed it to be at least a ten-minute walk or four-minute run with his guard down and showing fear. As he walked, he could hear what sounded like the scurrying of mice but much bigger—when he reached the third shrub, he realized they were rats the size of bulldogs. While three of them ran towards him, he could see one even had a small rusted sword protruding from its back. He shot at the first one three times hitting the thick skin on its back before it dropped, and steadied his gun to hit the next two in the head as they dropped close to his feet. That was when he felt the sharp sting of a bite on his left calf muscle. He turned to shoot it as it turned with him trying to pull him down. He grabbed the rusted short sword and stabbed it into the creatures' neck as he shot two more of them that almost reached him. He did not wait to see if there were more as he limped as fast as he could to the buildings still holding the sword.

He looked up, and overhead, he saw what looked like half-bat creatures with skinny human bodies flying in circles like vultures, waiting to eat a kill. He heard three loud thuds as one of the creatures fell from the sky with a large arrow through its chest, as he made a dash for the alley.

Between the buildings there were people on the stone streets. Some missing eyes, some their nose, some half their face was just bone.

Perhaps from leprosy or a flesh-eating drug addiction.

Not even the rats would eat them. He kept them at the point of his sword as he walked between buildings without windows only doors.

Then he came to a wall of wooden posts that looked like nothing but trees that had been stripped and poorly nailed together. He found a gate and banged on the door until a small window in it opened and the man asked what his business was.

"I am looking for passage to the River of Sorrows?"

"Well, you won't find one here. I am but a gatekeeper."

"Then how about you let me through your gate?"

"Of course, but it will cost you."

Az showed the man two pieces of copper leptas and his eyes lit up and he smiled.

"Come in, come in," said the man, quickly opening the door and closing it behind him.

Az handed the two coins to the man, and he looked Az over.

"Nope all in one piece, I see. Not falling apart, you are not. Yes you can enter, but that bite, you might want to get it looked at before it infects. Yes, yes before it infects."

"Where do I go for that?"

"That way." The man pointed down the only street of stone walls and doors then shook his head.

Az walked a bit and stopped to rest on a step of a building. He took a swig of his flask and poured the rest onto the bleeding bite wound on his leg.

He continued to walk until he heard a voice.

"How would you like to trade that rusty old sword in for something sharp?"

Az's head turned to see a hole cut into one of the buildings and a fat man standing behind the gate that covered it. It was one step up, and when he walked up that step, he could see behind the man an arsenal of swords, daggers, and some archery equipment.

"You have my ear," he replied back.

"Well, from the looks of it, that heavy old sword did not do the last person any good, and I am sure it will not do you any good either. Here, why not try this longsword for just two obols."

"Seems a little too big for me to be lugging around, what about that one?" Az pointed to one less than half its size.

"Good choice, good choice." The man put the blade on the counter. "For one obol I will also throw in this leather sheath and belt too?"

"That seems a little pricy for what it is, don't you think?"

In truth Az did not have a clue how much anything cost here. But from the eyes of the gatekeeper when he showed him the leptas, he knew this place did not have a lot of metal currency to go around.

"I like you, here is what I am going to do, stranger. The sword the sheath and two small daggers for an obol and that old sword, what do you say?"

The man grinned at him.

Az knew, at this point, if he said no, he would either insult him and not be able to trade there or end up paying twice as much for something he didn't want.

"Deal."

He put the obol on the counter with two fingers over it until the man placed his weapons onto it.

Az then grabbed the sword and sheath as he put the rusted one onto the counter. The two so-called daggers were nothing but two little thin banged pieces of metal, but they had a good sharp edge to them and Az slid them into the same sheath with the sword. Then Az released the lepta on the counter.

"I am in need of a healer. Would you know the way to one?"

"Of course, my friend, a little farther and you will be in the centre of town. Pass three streets and there you will find the temples of the elements. Beside the fire temple there is a good healer, just tell him Hephaestus sent you."

Az walked past the first two streets with nothing but shadows as his guide. Then on the third, there was a man lying at the side of the road and a set of stairs leading down to a red light.

"Pay the gatekeeper because you will never know when it is your turn," said a voice from the shadows—although there was no one else there. He bent down and placed two copper leptas in the man's hand and was confronted by an an all-too-familiar smell. It was as though the smoke from down the stairs had wrapped itself around him and was pulling him down. It took all of Az's strength to pull away—as though his eyes were bleeding and his lungs stopped breathing. While the pain in his leg throbbed letting him know he was still alive.

His trance ended when he felt a mist of water hitting his face, and he looked up to see a fountain of Poseidon with four winged horses coming out from the water and two mermaids looking up at him on either side. Above that, a large pillared square temple. He walked around it, and behind was a much larger fountain that spanned the entire distance of the back of the temple with Poseidon on a chariot pulled by twelve winged horses and at least fifty or more mermaids in the large basin in front of it. To his right was a building with a large iron gate around it, and behind that stood many statues of soldiers some of brass, iron, copper, and other metals. In the middle of the square was a pentagonal gazebo that had men and women wearing masks. Some masks bore horns, some the sun or moon, and some depicted creatures quite fitting for where he was. The clothing was quite revealing and provocative as they danced with their bodies touching one another to the beat of drums while people dressed as fauns played two horned flutes and danced around them.

Or at least he *thought* they were costumes.

There were ten staircases leading down from it, two at each point of the pentagon, and to the left of it was a forest with a long house at its entrance, and on its right hundreds of stone statues some of dwarves, elves, pixies, hobgoblins, deer, myrmidons, griffins, and fauns one that looked a lot like the one at Nagi's. In front of that building, a huge statue of Medusa. Then in the front was one more building with a fountain of lava instead of water, and above it a giant phoenix carved out of lava rock. All around the pentagon were little shops selling food, clothing, and trinkets as though the entire town was there in this one place.

Az could feel the heat of the lava and fire that was burning off of it. He looked to the left and right of the building behind the phoenix and had a fifty-fifty chance of picking the correct way. At first, he thought to go right but then went left instead. He walked until he could smell the all-too-familiar scent of blood and looked at the white tent. Inside, the floor was stained red, and a blue woman stopped him and asked how she could help?

Az rolled up his pant leg and pointed to the bite that was turning black, she walked over to a box with small glass bottles and pulled one out that was no bigger than his pinky finger.

"Six leptas."

Az handed her an obol and she gave him the bottle with no change.

"Thirteen drops will do."

He right away dropped thirteen drops in his hand and rubbed it onto his wound. It didn't heal right away like he was hoping, but the blackness turned pink.

"What way to the River of Sorrows?" he asked.

She pointed to the forest and said, "Once through the temple of wood, there is a graveyard that keeps out the Jorōgumo ghosts that could shapeshift into spiders. Then there is a field, then another forest that will take you to your river."

Az thanked her and walked out into the forests.

- What A Tangled Web We Weave

The leaves crackled under his feet, and no longer warmed by the heat of the phoenix fountain, he could see his breath, and the farther he walked the more the mist surrounded him. He drew his sword, as it sparked off a tombstone, and he could see he was now surrounded by hundreds of crosses with a circle around the middle—Irish crosses. He felt the interwoven snakelike patterns on the stone and wondered if it was to honour the snake god and cult. He looked down and picked one of the purple flowers that grew on the graves around him. His eyes were now accustomed to the dark, and he could see stones of circles and ghostlike faces that looked as though they were screaming mixed with the crosses that he assumed were the legion of the Jorōgumo. Az looked up and could see the point on the cliff above him that looked as though there was a face carved in it looking down at him.

He entered into the darkness of the treeline ahead, and for an Earth day walked through the forest with nothing but the noise under his feet to keep him company. Then he could smell smoke and walked until he could see a small twinkle of firelight. As he approached, he could see six young women standing around the fire. Their skin looked soft and smooth and they had long black hair and wore silk dresses so tight he could see the sharp angle of their hips and the small pert shape of their breasts.

They looked at him and smiled; Az smiled back.

The first one put her hand on his face and he could not stop staring into her round eyes. Another put her hand on his stomach and walked behind him while he put his hand out to feel the soft silk of her dress. His hand slid across her back. One put her hand on his leg and stroked his inner thigh then moved again to his back. The next one did the same until they were all spinning around him.

Then a voice. English.

—There is something crawling on you—

And he stopped looking at their eyes and looked down to see the shiny white silk strands that were beginning to wrap around his body. It was too tight for him to pull his sword, and so he took one of the small daggers out of the sheath with his pinky and sliced thought the silk threads, cutting upwards and freeing himself. In the same fluid motion, with his thumb on the butt of the handle, he spun it from right to left slicing into three of their necks—blood poured across his hand. The other three ran up the tree as though they were running along the ground, and when Az looked up, he could see hundreds of cocoons hanging from the tree. Then a small spider fell on his arm and bit him. He slapped it off as he ran towards where the river should be.

It did not kill him, the venom, although he wished it had. The trees looked like they were breathing and around them dragons of light flew between the trunks. He knew he was in a hallucinogenic state and running would only cause an injury. He looked behind him to see if anything was following him.

A bird flew from the ground into the trees and it sounded like it screamed at him. Instead of running, he crouched down and sat perfectly still, listening for the sound of crunching leaves on the ground, but heard none. Then he looked up and listened for the creak of branches above him, but again nothing. He knew it was now only a matter of him being able to deal with himself as he walked slowly through the forest.

Two to three Earth hours later, the dragons had all left him, and he came to the river with a stone port and stood there looking around. He saw a lantern hanging from a dead tree bough and touched it with his finger—a flame lit the wick inside the glass. A minute later, he could see a light floating along the water, and as it approached him, a decrepit wooden vessel docked along the rocks. It was an ancient wooden canoe and in its stern stood a hooded figure with a long pole he'd used to push the canoe along the water. In the bow was a lit lantern that hung over the water on a pole and behind it a metal can. Az stepped into the boat and held two copper leptas in his hand.

"Erebus," he said.

The figure pointed to the can with a boney hand. Az heard the coins clatter against other coins in the bottom of the can. He sat in the canoe as the lantern he lit went out with a gust of wind and looked at the water and watched the bodies floating by, until they came to a large black stone castle that the river flowed around.

The ferryman stopped port side at a small unmanned stone wharf below the drawbridge that had a lit lantern hanging from a pole over the water. As Az stood up to exit, the ferryman put out his hand, and Az handed him an obol. The ferryman handed him a piece of paper with a red symbol on it of a bull. He walked up a small stone staircase that extruded from the base of the castle up to the drawbridge where three black-haired Votea stood guard. One on each side of the gate and one in the middle. Az handed the one at the top of the stairs the paper, and the Votea moved to one side to let him in.

In the courtyard of the castle there was a masquerade ball taking place. No one seemed to even notice he was there. They only danced, never touching one another, but always looking into each other's eyes with one hand in the air at shoulders height.

He walked by an entire table of fruits and cakes and things that made his mouth water, but in his stomach, he felt no hunger as we walked by it. He walked into a room on the right that was full of medieval torture devices. Along a wall was an arsenal of weapons that could outfit an army of thousands. One piece stood as though out of place—a mirror: and in front of that mirror was the helm of darkness an Illyrian helmet with plumes of black horse hair resting on a stand with a skull at the top. Az picked it up and could feel as though he were made of energy, and as he placed it on his head, his body disappeared, clothing and all. When he touched the skull with his hand it too disappeared, and he walked back out to the courtyard again with no one even looking. He walked to the tower on the right of the castle, and lifted a key from the belt of a sleeping guard and unlocked the wooden door he'd been guarding.

He climbed the circle stairs up the tower and, at the top, found a room and could see the princess through the small hole in the door. He slid the key into the hole and heard the click as it opened. She was standing with her back to him, looking out the window with a pomegranate broken open on the windowsill. By the time Az was behind her, she had eaten three pomegranate seeds and she turned to look when she felt a breeze behind her but could see no one. Az, stunned by the beauty of her face, put his hand on her right shoulder.

He appeared to her then.

"Shhh princess, I was sent here by Queen Demeter to rescue you."

She only nodded. Az took her by the hand and led her down the stairs and through the ball as everyone stood there not moving for the music had stopped playing. He walked out the gate past the three Votea and down the little set of stairs to see that the charon was still waiting for him. He stood in the boat and helped the princess step on. Then he placed two leptas into the can as the ferryman pushed off and started down the River of Sorrows. Within minutes they heard a loud horn blow from the castle and four horsemen on black horses rode across the drawbridge as one stared down at them to see an empty boat. A hundred of the half-bat creatures flew from the top of the castle.

The ferryman stopped at the forest once again. This time he did not hold out his hand for a tip and only pointed into the dark woods. Az could not tell if it was a reflection from the lantern or the eyes of the ferryman were fire.

He did not let go of the princess and did not stop running for fear that she would be lost into the thick mist. He could hear dogs howling and barking in the distance behind them as they ran through the cemetery to the temples of the elements where there was not a soul in sight. The water in the fountains did not run, but the lava and fire spewed upwards around the phoenix. Even at the wooden wall, there was no one as he pulled upwards the latch that kept the gate locked and closed it behind him, hearing the click, knowing he could have just damned them both. But again, there was no one and nothing but the fog. When he reached the wall, he banged on the wooden doors, but no one answered until he took off the helmet, revealing the princess.

As the bat creatures began to dive, he could hear the thud noise of the ballistae as the doors flew opened and one of the creatures grabbed the helmet from his hand as he was being pulled by the large brown-haired Votea through the gatehouse where centaurs were fighting off the bats and closing the door behind him as he fell from exhaustion while being dragged off.

He awoke to the sound of Nagi's voice informing him that his ship was ready—he wondered what was real and what was a dream. He received a royal escort to the ships in a carriage with Nagi who said the queen's ships were ready to sail, the

Manat, the *Al-Lat*, and the flagship *Al-Uzza*. When he asked Nagi what happened to Princess Persephone Nagi told him she was to be betrothed to Hades and that the wedding would be in six moons.

The carriage door opened as a guard held his hand out for Az to step down.

"You are not coming with me, Nagi?"

"No, my young friend, this is as far as my journey takes me. Safe travels."

"You too, Nagi."

As he walked up the plank of the *Al-Uzza*, the captain and two officers were there to greet him.

"Welcome aboard, Az. I am Captain Moor, and we have been expecting you. Officer Fath, here, will bring you to your quarters."

Then the captain turned to the officer on his right.

"First Officer Tabit, have my ship out of this port before the surf takes her."

"Yes sir," Tabit said then started yelling orders to the rest of the crew.

7

Origon

Aboard the ship, Az was treated as the guest he was. An out of place checkers piece on a chess board. He spent most of his time just staring out into the bluest of blue oceans. He thought of the old man Nagi alone and wanted to return to him but knew he must go on. Many of the things Nagi said to him that sounded like passing of the time conversations now rang in his head. So often ending in, *then you have not learned anything yet.*

The three ships sailed like a flock as the *Al-Uzza* kept point. For two hours between each moon they would drop the sails, while Az and the officers of the ship would eat and discuss their bearings. During one of these meals Captain Moor turned to Az.

"This journey reminds me of a story I heard as a boy. A frog is sitting on a lily pad close to the shore of a pond.

A scorpion appears on the shore and asks the frog if he would carry him to the other side. 'No,' the frog replies. And when the scorpion asks why, the frog says, 'Because you are a scorpion and will sting me with your tail.' But the scorpion says, 'If I sting you with my tail then we will both drown, so I assure you I will not.' And so the frog relents and lets the scorpion ride on his back. When they reach the middle of the pond the scorpion stings the frog in his back, paralyzing him. Before they drown the frog says, 'Why did you do that? Now we will both drown.' The scorpion's only reply was 'Because I am a scorpion.'"

"I assure you, Captain, I am no scorpion."

"Perhaps not, but I know where we are going is."

The ship saw land after two and a half months of water and waves. Nothing more than a kick of a stone to Az—in space one can travel for hundreds of years before reaching a destination and every hundred years you were cycled through with some of the spaceships crew to be thawed out from the cryogenic status for up to two years to make sure there was no permanent damage to the *cargo* as the ship's crew called the passengers.

They docked at a small two-boat dock on the Island of Origon. It was nothing in comparison to the docks of Annwn. On one side there was what looked like a frigate, and the other side was where the *Al-Uzza* docked as the *Manat* and the *Al-Lat* dropped anchor so that their cannons could reach the shoreline. The crew was fully armed and stood at port side with their guns pointed down off the ship. Captain Moor and First Officer Tabit walked down the plank first with Az behind them.

Standing on the docks were five immortals of the Golden Army, waiting in long brown robes with large hoods covering their heads. But five was more than enough to terrify the ship's crew. Az could see the one standing in front was a woman with a dark completion and black hair protruding from the hood and behind her four men. They looked so young he could not believe this was them or that they could be so feared.

"We do not welcome uninvited company," said the woman.

Then Officer Tabit spoke up in a loud voice. "Her royal majesty Queen Demeter honours our peace alliance with the Kings of Origon and has brought many spices, furs, gifts, and slaves from the mainland. She has also granted safe passage to the messenger Sir Azuse. Presented by Captain Moor of the *Al-Uzza*."

"I am Talah," said the immortal standing in front. "We have been expecting you, Az, for quite some time. We accept your gifts Captain Moor. Please have the slaves released and the cargo unloaded onto the docs. The townspeople will bring the goods from there. Your ships and crew are welcome to the town to gather supplies and rest before your voyage home."

"The grace of the Kings of Origon is truly unmatched in this world," replied the captain.

"Come Az," Talah said and motioned with her hand while the other four immortals turned and walked away.

As they walked through the town, talking to each other, Az could not understand them until the words sounded like broken English then finally English that he could understand. It was just covered in a thick accent from their mumble and so many years away from anyone else from Earth.

When they reached the large pyramid, Az saw the USS *Wildfire* an identical ship to the USS *Spirit* sitting outside of the pyramid.

"Your friends arrived some time ago, assuming you were all dead," said Talah.

"So where is the crew?"

"Would you like to see them?" Talah asked. "It's almost feeding time."

Az could not wait to have some food that was not from the *Al-Uzza* cook. They walked through the gates of the massive walls surrounding the giant pyramid, and the five immortals stood around a hole in the ground just inside of the main courtyard. Az walked to the edge and looked down, making sure he was not beside someone who might push him in. There were three people chained to a wall, and as a door opened, the flight crew and troopers rushed through it like animals slashing and gnawing at the people on the wall. Az recognized them as the second ship's crew by their half-torn clothes and military tattoos on the skin.

"Why have you done that to them?" he asked.

"I assume you mean your soldiers," said Talah, "and not the people they are violently massacring?"

"Yes."

"They asked to be immortalized. How were we to say no? You see, Az, when they took the blood into them, the thirst was so overwhelming they tore through the town feeding until their bellies were full. Then they continued to drink, poisoning our crops and turning them. We had to put down half our town. That is why we are thankful for the slaves that were brought to restock the town. I am sure they are simply Queen Demeter prisoners or a jail that was cleaned out. Either way, we will quickly discern what ones will cause trouble here.

"How did you really become like this?" Az asked.

Talah stood there a moment as if in contemplation. "You see, a long time ago, on Earth, a tomb was found, and the blood of a true ancient was uncovered. However, the body was only partially decomposed, and there were fleas feeding on its corpse. Once released into the world, they spread the disease. It was known by many names, the most famous of which was the bubonic or black plague. It killed over half a billion people over the centuries.

"That was until our war, then the scientists were able to extract the stem cell gene from it and inoculated us with it. Perhaps we would have gone mad like them were it not for the war. Or perhaps we did go mad—after all, we are all children of the disease. That's how the life extension therapy treatments were started. A small amount of the gene was altered and perfected. That's why, after that war, everyone stopped dying naturally. Now come, you must meet our leader Lord Nemth."

They walked into a room with an oval table and a man sitting at its head. As they entered the man spoke.

"It has been a long time since a sage from the mainland has come to visit us here. I am the Emperor Nemth, and this is my realm. What brings you here?"

"I am Azuse known as Az. I am here on official business from Isaac. You have been reenlisted and summoned for duty."

"Isaac," he said. "Now that is a name I have not heard in some centuries. However, you present yourself with more knowledge than your predecessors. Perhaps I was not mistaken with my first assumption of you, but we will see."

"Is this the Temple of Orgona?" Az asked.

"No. This is the Tomb of Haljkent, a loyal guard, and one of five temples dedicated to the dead god Orgona. You see, for one single god to die, it is almost impossible to find a tomb for them. There have been maybe three since the beginning of time."

"Have you found the tomb yet?"

"No, but we are sure it is here. This is not the largest of the tombs."

"So where is the rest of the Golden Army?"

"Here on this island lives some of the Golden Army," said Emperor Nemth. "But we will discuss more at dinner. Please, feel free to look around until then, as our guest."

He wandered around the giant tomb and through all the corridors he could find. The immortals were a very quiet people. They walked around and stared out at the nothingness around them, not even noticing Az was there. Until one who *looked* younger than him—who had long red hair with a gray strip in her bangs—stopped and addressed him.

"Hello Azuse, my name is Nilhal, it is a beautiful place here isn't it?"

"Yes, it is. The artwork is amazing, but what I don't understand are the hieroglyphics the way the stone is notched out around them and they are not notched into the stone."

"How observant of you, Azuse. You see in most other worlds, due to greed and the fear of knowledge, the hieroglyphics are always chiseled off and new hieroglyphics are chiseled deep into the stone in their place."

"And what of that which was once written?" asked Az.

"It is lost forever. A gift from the creators easily taken away. However, you will see the most interesting thing is not here, but in the sand. It is the far pyramid to the west where the sun dies to be reborn anew. That is where you will find what you are not looking for."

"And what is it that you think I am not looking for?"

"The gods and their return, some of the hieroglyphics here indicate that that temple holds some kind of key." said Nilhal. "No one has ever been there, and it hurts us to even walk in that direction."

Az and Nilhal walked back to the dining hall where they sat down at a table of ten immortals plus Nemth. Az sat at the chair beside Nemth and listened as they began to talk about Earth, watching as the food was all brought out and set onto the table in such an abundance that it could not possibly all be eaten.

Nilhal, who sat beside Az, took but a small plate of food and a glass of the red wine. Others too took only small portions, barely making a dent in the vast feast.

"What of all the wasted food after this meal?" said Az.

"Food is never wasted here," said Nilhal. "It will be put into soups and feed in the town square for those who have no food—like the town's new arrivals that came with you, while they adapt to their new home."

At that moment. Nemth called for the attention of all those around the table.

"So we are asked once again to save Earth from itself."

"And why should we go to help a planet that abandoned us?" asked Talah.

"They did not abandon us," said an immortal named Airistal. "We abandoned them. We are feared, and that is why we are needed again."

"This will be the greatest battle ever," said Nemth. "And we will have an adversary that will rival all."

"It is better to have truly lived for one day," said one named Brial, "than to only stay alive for many years."

"You will all ride off to your regions and inform the rest of the immortals of the arrival," said Nemth, "and we will commence again on the sixth of the large moons."

After Nemth's speech, the ale was brought out, and they drank and feasted as though there would be no tomorrow. Az wandered into the courtyard where they brought in dancers to appease them, and he watched as they danced so symbolically the way they swayed and moved as if possessed by the same force. Like smoke in the air, the colours of their dresses hypnotized his eyes. The silhouettes of their naked bodies under the see-through colours had his mind pressed. He thought of the voyage here, of water and waves, and now here watching a thing of beauty. They must have spent their entire lives practicing to dance like that, and when Nilhal told Az that one of the dancers desired him, he could hardly hold back his smile.

Here it seemed there was nothing but days, and in space, nothing but nights. That alone was enough to drive someone mad.

Az spent more and more of the passing time talking with Nilhal. Even when they talked about nothing at all, it was like they talked about everything. The universe, interplanetary worlds, and all of the religions they would have to offer. Az spent so much time talking about different religions in the Milky Way alone, he was beginning to think they were all one religion of fragmented pieces that were pulled apart, and in his mind, he was beginning to put them all back together to see the bigger picture—much in the same way the religions on Earth were pieced together many years ago. His eyes became hazy from the wine, and his mind became opened to the light.

–The Spider and the Fly

One of the immortals' duties was to pass judgment on the people of their regions, and Lord Nemth requested that

Nilhal and Azuse go to a small farming village not far from there where a body was found.

Upon arriving to the village, they were brought by the town sheriff to the town butcher shop's basement. The walls were lined with cork and it was cool enough that you could almost see your breath. The body was laying on the only table, and there were some pigs hanging upside down on hooks around it.

Az walked up to the body, looked at the wound and stuck his figure in it. Then asked to see the weapons of the area and they brought him to the village armoury. He walked past a line of swords hanging by their guard and moved his figures along the hilts listening to them chime as the tips clinked together. At the end was a pile of spears leaning against the wall, and he picked one up and turned to Nilhal and the Sheriff.

"These are all weapons for a soldier not a farmer, what tools would a farmer have as a weapon?" Az walked out still carrying the spear in his hand.

They brought him to a barn containing all the tools used by an old farming family that was a pillar of the community. The farmers welcomed them and the barn had many different bladed tools from shovels to pitchforks to some he had never even seen before.

He requested a slaughtered pig be brought and hung in the barn on some of the chains hanging from the rafters. Then he stabbed it with the spear and showed the rounded wound; then a pitchfork and showed how it would leave only little holes. A hoe left a huge gash, and a knife, a straight cut into the body. Then he picked up a small handheld scythe and showed how it left the curved angle cut into the body.

"This is the tool of your reaper. Find his scythe and you will have found your killer."

Nilhal turned to the sheriff and said, "Have all the farmers summoned and bring their scythes."

A small moon later, the farmers were gathered, and each was given a different colour cloth around their necks that was also used to mark the different scythes placed on a table in another room.

The three stood there looking at the almost identical scythes.

"Are you sure these are all of them?" Az asked.

"It is not a cheap tool," said the sheriff, "and we are having the guards search their houses as we speak. This should be all of them. But how will you know which one killed the man?"

Az looked at the table for a minute, then went into another room to collect his thoughts as he ate some ham sitting on the table from lunch. As he sat at the small bench and table, he stared out the window as a fly kept flying around him and hitting the window.

He thought about how on a ship or on a planet, flies were everywhere. But no matter where they were, they had one thing in common. They liked to eat meat as though the universe used them as a quick way to break down dead flesh.

He went back out to the room with the scythes and asked for glass panels to create a case around the table with the scythes in them. He then asked to have flies collected and brought to him.

Within an Earth hour, the case was completed, and thirty flies had been collected into a jar.

He had two of the guards lift the glass case as Az opened the lid and placed the jar of flies inside. Then the guards lowered the case back onto the table.

They quickly flew around and after some time they landed on only one scythe and began eating.

Az then pointed to the scythe and the blue ribbon around its handle. "There is your reaper."

Nilhal ordered for the man to be hanged, and they hung him in the village square but not long enough to kill him. They then carted him away to where Nilhal and Az were waiting, and she brought him back to the tomb for his real execution.

On the first of the large moon's covering the sun, Az was walking with Nilhal in the cooled air, and she turned and looked at Az in the eyes.

"I must leave and return to my people," said Nilhal, "and inform the other immortals there of the meeting."

"Your presence here will be missed," said Az.

"I am sure you will find something to do in my absence," said the immortal.

Az nodded. "The pyramid to the west. I must see what is there."

"I will have some animals loaded with supplies for your journey at first light," said Nilhal. "Remember this, you will have all the supplies you need to make it there. But there is no way to take the supplies you need to make it home. Is this journey into the desert for the information you seek worth risking your life?"

"If it is vital to the mission," said Az, "then it is always more important than a soldier's life. Information wins wars. It is the blood of the soldiers that the information is written with."

8

The Sands of Time

In the morning there were four animals packed with supplies and tied to one another. As a species it looked like a cross between a rhinoceros and a small dinosaur. Only Nilhal was standing in front of them, waiting for Az though a dozen men from town stood nearby.

"Nilhal, are there more of these beasts available?"

"They are called talicks, and no, I am afraid not."

Az handed her a purse of coins. "Then I want these four loaded up with twice the goods they now carry, they certainly look more than capable of bearing it."

Nilhal only smiled and handed the coins to one of the men from town.

After about an Earth hour the men returned with carts of goods. Az picked through the carts and had the things loaded onto the talicks then took one rifle he grabbed from the USS *Wildfire* earlier with him.

Nilhal stared up at Az on his talick.

"Well then, you are all set, are you not?"

"How will I find it in nothing but sand?" Az asked.

"The hieroglyphs say, You do not find it, for it will find you, if you are one of the chosen. The desert is only a desert for those who do not understand. When you begin to understand, the desert will no longer be a desert, and when you fully understand, then the desert will be a desert again.

"In the meantime," she said, "follow the wind. It always flows west and will lead you there."

"You have become a good friend, Nilhal. I look forward to seeing you again on my return."

Az rode into the sun, wearing light robes that blocked the relentless rays but allowed the wind to pass through.

After three Earth months, one of the talicks fell from heat and exhaustion, at least two months sooner than Nilhal said the first one should fall. Az took the rifle and shot it in the head, and the other talicks began to eat their fallen comrade, starting with its stomach as its guts spilled across the sand. The talicks were herbivores when they had a supply of water and were scavengers when without water to absorb the water the other animal held within.

"Better you eat him then me, tiny," Az said as he smacked the one he was riding on the side of the leg.

He set up his tent a distance away from them since he did not want to be in the way of a feeding frenzy for fear of being stepped on or worse. The days there proved hot and harsh while the nights from the moons were cold and just as dry. He unloaded a lot of the goods to just leave there in the desert in hopes that it would allow the beasts a longer lifespan with less weight to carry. Trying to decide what to take and what to leave can drive any man crazy as the whole process is decision after decision.

When the beasts began to eat from the backside of the fallen talick, he would spend most of the day in the empty stomach of the animal. It was the only cool place—as if it was air conditioned—and he found it also kept the meat inside along the ribs fresh. He would cut off a slice an inch thick and cook it by burning some of the fat to save his rations—those animals had a lot of fat with which to retain water. He did this until the meat turned and became very soft and smelled something fierce. He knew not to move his tent too far away from the corpse or he would never find his way back through the sand to them.

Az travelled again, stopping every time one died, and by the passing of the second one, he started drinking its blood to save on water.

The last one fell just within sight of the pyramid. Az jerked some of the meat to make it smaller and lighter in hopes it would keep it from rotting. As he walked away, he wanted to grab all the water, but water is a tricky thing, it's mass versus distance. Is it better to be sweating out from the water that is being carried or to just carry less water? It did not take long for him to feel like he was going mad. His eyes burned at the sight of his destination. His lips cracked, and his face began to scab from the sun and sand beating it.

His body had grown thin and light, and he had started to see little specks of glowing silver lights flashing around him, fading and flaring like sparkling fireflies in the night—only if he tried to catch them, they weren't there. Just another part of the mirage of hell and sand.

He thought at one point it was just sand in the air, but with only a light breeze that felt more like a hand on his back guiding him, he knew it wasn't true.

He felt as though death were a part of him now and that his long life was finally over. But the sparkling lights would not have it so. They became part of him—he breathed them in, not with his lungs but throughout his entire body. They fuelled each of his steps, and he began to come up with the notion that the pure essence of life itself was around him. The energy of the soul that is faded away through time from the body. It was the fire that burned behind everything. It was the living and the dead, the stars and planets and everything in between.

He began to see the spirits of the dead guiding him; faces would appear, then whole bodies. Then it showed as though he was walking through time, whole cities and people rising and falling, from ships that fly into space, then to planes, then tanks, then only soldiers, then knights with swords and horsemen, then back again as the building changed shape and people walked through him as though he were not even there. He saw planets and stars being created and destroyed.

But this was not the first time he had these dreams—only this time he was not flowing with it, he was only watching. Then it all stopped at once, and he fell under the shade of a tree and began eating the fruit that had fallen onto the ground and drank from the water. However, in his mind, it was only sand in front of him, and he had gone mad but did not care.

He awoke on a bed within a room in a bamboo hut and tried to get up, but he was too weak to move. A purple-skinned woman walked through the door carrying a basin of cool water and began to wash him down. He had never set eyes on the Agoti before—other than in his dreams. She smelled so heavenly like jasmine and vanilla. He tried to talk, but his throat was stripped, and all he could taste was his own blood with every breath.

The woman poured a light pink drink into his mouth, and he choked as he tried to drink a sip of it.

"It is a nectar from the palm tree," she said to him in a soothing soft voice. "It will heal you until you can eat again."

The shining dots sparkled around her, and it was as if there were a bluish-purple glow that steamed off from her. He tried to speak, and she only put one figure over his mouth to stop him before he even said a word. Every time he tried to speak, they shook their head no or put a finger over his mouth. He began to feel as though he were trapped inside his own head as his thoughts began to race faster and faster with every day he did not speak. Eventually, his thoughts slowed again and he did not feel the need to speak.

It took three months until Az had the strength to walk again. There were only the purple women there, no children or men. He tried to be aroused when looking at their beauty, but around them, it seemed impossible. Their beautiful smell and soft skin were only surpassed by the tranquility of it all. There was a natural spring that shot up out of the ground and fed the trees, the fruits, and the grass around the pyramid—a perfect oasis in the nothingness.

Oh, how he'd missed the smell and touch of soft grass; it might as well have been cotton or clouds under his feet.

He often would spend his time by the trickle of the creek bed just lying on the grass under the shade of a tree, listening to the way the water just flowed out from it over the smoothed rocks as the women would bring him the sweet pink cold nectar.

The sparkles began to fade from his eyes, but never left completely. He could move his hand as they appeared and change the course of the wind if he wished to. Finally, he ventured into the sands of time pyramid. Inside was a huge domed room, and he stood in awed amazement at a self-floating diagram of the pendulum at the centre of the Milky Way, but it showed more. It showed the history of the species that came to see it. He realized what it was all about the Mayan calendar and the year 2012.

It was always looked at as only one day that came and went, but the true Mayan calendar was in a circle. It only depicted larger calendars, showing the arrival of the Europeans then the war of 1812, then the world wars. The year 2012, the year that the Pegasus Galaxy home of the Votea Royal family and the Andromeda home to the Chool Empire came close enough to each other that the Milky Way Galaxy became a bridge between the two giants and began a war that Earth would play an important future role in by 2712 when Earth too joined in the battle of the heavens. Az watched how the Votea were represented in orange for every planet they took and the Chool were represented in red for every planet they took control of. There was one little blue dot right where the Earth was. Then it showed Proxima b turn blue, then a planet home to the Malinnes, and from there quickly the entire Milky Way galaxy turned blue—and the red and orange dots were pushed back to their respective galaxies.

Az stared at the giant star in the middle and the string of planets that was the pendulum. It connected to a dozen different galaxies in the universe other than the Milky Way. But it never touched the Andromeda galaxy or Pegasus as if it travelled through the middle of the black hole. Most black holes were like wormholes in space as though they were roots to a tree. Many different black holes would suck in light and everything else, and on the other side, one would shoot out light deep into space. Here it was a giant bubble in the middle, the start of the Big Bang. The star was the closed gates to the time before time, where it all began and one day would all end. On the floor, he noticed small bumps that he scanned with his wrist comp.

They spelled out "judgment day" in ancient Greek and other dead languages.

He looked at how close the hands of time were to the Milky Way and knew it could only be a hundred years or so at the centre until they reach it or less. But a hundred years in the centre could be thousands where Earth sat.

Az took off his T2700 and stood it directly under the pendulum. He pointed it up at the star, the tear in the universe, a gate to heaven that will only be opened when the wars of the angels are over. He turned on his real-time recorder and left the building, hoping the transmission would be able to be picked up from their moon base.

—What Is Heaven to You?

When he walked out of the temple, the women were standing on both sides of the door, staring at him as he walked past them. He knew they did not go in there, and he shouldn't have either, at least not if he wished to stay in their garden.

He walked with the sun on his back into the desert between them, and as he left the grass, one of the women gave him a sack with corked coconuts in it and kissed him on the cheek. Az threw it over his shoulder and kept walking into the desert.

He stopped occasionally to have a sip of the pink nectar contained in the coconuts, and when he finished one, he would crack it open and eat small pieces of coconut. He walked back to where he had left his last talick and supplies, but the desert had already swallowed it whole.

The glow started again, and they turned into faces of the dead—some who he'd known, some he had killed—and sometimes they talked with him. At one point, he swore he was in the presence of the dead God.

When the sun hid behind a moon, he missed the heat, and when it returned, he missed the cold. He wanted to return to the safety of his bed surrounded by the Agoti. He missed the days laying in the grass and the sound of the trickling stream. But all decisions good or bad come with consequences.

When he returned to the Tomb of Haljkent, he did not know if he had been in the desert for forty months or forty years? He walked through the front of the temple and into the courtyard. It was full of the immortals who all turned and stared at him. Az did not stop until he was in front of Lord Nemth.

"Emperor Nemth, this is only part of the once great gold army. If we are to succeed, we will need to forge the Golden Sword of the Immortals back into one."

"The rest of the immortals have left long ago to the city of Gomorrah where they will not leave their lavish lifestyle so easily," said Emperor Nemth. "If you return with *Cronus* and prove yourself worthy, then we will all return to Earth together."

"I accept your quest Lord Nemth and will return with *Cronus*."

"And who else will volunteer to take on this journey of yours?" asked Emperor Nemth.

The ten kings of the realm stepped forward, and Nilhal looked at Az and smiled.

"And do the Lords all agree?" asked Nemth.

The rest of the immortals said, "Aye."

"And who opposes this journey?"

The room stayed silent.

"Then let it begin," said Nemth, "and you will mend the Golden Sword into one."

Emperor Nemth walked into the dining hall, and the ten kings of their realms followed. Az now recognized that he was an ambassador from Earth, and when he looked at them, the age of the immortals was now a glow coming from them. He could look one minute and see flesh and blood and in the next it was as though they were pure energy radiating upwards creating a shape that looked like crowns on the top of their heads, and he could see their knowledge was what they stared at as they walked passed.

After the next moon, the ten kings boarded the freight with Az and began their sea voyage.

When they reached the shores of the mainland, they did not unload anything. Brial, the third immortal, put his hand on the captain's shoulder and nodded his head. Then they loaded into two of the lifeboats and were rowed to shore by the crew.

They walked along the shoreline, and the ship sailed off, leaving them stranded there. When day turned to night, Brial pointed to the Sirius star and how it looked like the star was crashing into the ground.

"There, that is where *Cronus* lies imprisoned in the tallest mountain looking down on us all. We must climb only the mountain where the Sirius star touches the tip. There, at the top, will stand two golden statues of women, they are the wives of Orion. You must walk between the golden statues, and if you are a son or daughter of Orion, you will be allowed to pass into the halls of thunder. If you are not of pure blood, you will die! For the statues will come alive with the fury of the wives, and their eyes will burn your soul until you are nothing but dust and ash."

"Well then, at first light we will begin our journey," Az said. "However, who says there is still a ship there, and if there is, how will we know it can still fly?"

"Azuse, your youthful ways amuse me. It is not a matter of the ship being there but of your willingness to walk through the gates of the golden status into the hall of thunder."

When the darkness of the moon began to subside, they walked for two Earth days, finally stopping in a town for rest and finding themselves in one of the small-town pubs to escape the heat. Az looked directly at a Votea, sitting alone at a table drinking a rather large glass of beer. The kings sat at their own table, and Az sat at the table of the Votea—the enormous wolf–and looked up at him.

"Leave my sight if you value your life," said the beast.

"So the slaves can talk?"

"We are the keepers of the gods."

"The gods are but enchanted relics," said Az, "dizzied by their own ignorance of immortality and ability to manipulate matter."

He felt a small amount of fear just saying that and shrugged it off quickly as the Votea caught a scent with his nose.

"They are as old as time itself," said the Votea. "They hold the key to the pendulum."

"And *Cronos* then is the star's bridge to all other galaxies," said Az, "the father of time?"

"Yes, but who says that beyond the bridge of light there are not far worse things than we can imagine, and that when they return, they only reset the natural balance to all. Your kind is too young to remember when it was you who were slaves to the gods. But I remember, I remember when the humans were first brought here."

"Our kind has risen past physical gods," said Az. "We know of the spirit known as the one God, the true God that seeded the womb known as creation. It holds our souls so we may be reborn again. It is said, in time of war, we are reborn with the memories of our past lives so we may finish the war that we started."

"And do you?" said the dog. "Do you remember your past, human?"

"My name is Azuse," Az said. "And no, I do not! Though I do remember a dream so real to me that I am not sure it is not a memory at all."

"Azuse," the Votea said as if weighing the syllables. "My name is Anamanto. So Azuse, when did you first have this dream?"

"I only ever had the dream once as though it was before I was born."

"And tell me of this dream so vivid it is a memory."

Az took a long drink of his beer. "There was a time when life was noncorporeal, just a feeling and colours, and though colours could not be seen, they could be felt. It was a time of healing so that the souls of many may rest. However, there was a noise."

"Did you make this noise?" asked Anamanto.

"No, but I heard it. Others mocked the noises, and the noise echoed and travelled back and forth like water ripples in a rain drenched puddle. The noise became words, and the words became sentences, and the sentences became much more, they became conversations. Allowing us to know there was more out there than ourselves."

"And in this time of nothingness of colour and fog, what did you do?"

"I travelled like water flowing in babbling brooks, and then I stopped at a rock."

"A rock," said Anamanto. "So, there was material objects there?

"No, not a rock exactly. It was a strong invisible force that the water—that *we*—flowed around it to never notice it was there."

"And at this rock, what did you find?"

"I found something older than the nothing," said Az.

"And what did you do with this *time* you discovered?"

"I stared into it with blinding eyes, until it talked, and it told me of a test! A test of life, death, beginnings and ends, a time of pain, pleasure, touch, sound, an ending taste that would seem endless. Where you must hold your soul together and keep your mind at one with the time and vast space while travelling through the light, a test of time."

"Did you understand what it meant?"

"I understood that it had already been through this path that I was to take," Az said. "But little did I know we were all about to take it. Then he taught me of silence and not to crave the distraction of noise. So I meditated and slipped back into the brooks again. Only, this time, my conversations were thin as if there were more to say with fewer words.

"A following gathered around me, too big to know it was a wave, until we all came crashing on the sleeping stones as the wave broke across them and awoke the end with millions of questions as the stones became buried in them. That was until the stones broke open, revealing a door or a hole or a light and a noise said, 'Enough,' and there was silence.

"Immaterial beings were staring into everything—or nothing—and no one wanted to go through it. But I remembered that test of time, a way to become one like them and I said, 'Don't worry. I have this all figured out. Let's go!' And like a moth to a flame, I was born."

"And is that where your story ends, and you begin?"

"No," said Az. "I ran with the stars until the stars stood still and did not want to run anymore, and there it began—war after war, lifetimes of death making the spirit incrementally stronger. Until I had my fill of anger, and I fell into a deep despair of what I had become, and there, there I sat in the darkness until the age of machines, and I travelled as a spirit, guiding a group of young soldiers, only revealing myself as they died. And at the end of the war I was born again to die again with new strength to be born again."

"When you were born into this life," said Anamanto, "what was the first thing that you heard?"

"I was staring into the sun in a forest and I heard. 'How did he get there?' And another voice said, 'There is nothing we can do about it now.' That was the last time the sun spoke to me."

Anamanto looked at Az and said, "You speak with age for such a young body. You are welcome to sit at my table and take part in drinking of the spirits tonight."

In the moon's passing, Az awoke feeling unprofessional with the dream he told. However, nothing was said at breakfast to accompany the pounding of his head. If there was only one thing Az had learned, no matter what planet he is on, the coffee bean, chocolate bean, poppies, and aspirin had always beaten him there. Not to mention wine, and Oh, did Az ever miss a cold carbonated beer.

He walked towards the fireplace picked up the steel pot beside the hot coals and poured himself a cup of coffee. The entire party was already awake and sitting at the tables. He looked at the ten kings with the cup in his hand.

He then looked to his left and saw Anamanto standing there. Az looked up at him.

"When do you plan on sleeping?" he asked.

"When you are all gone, so I will join you until you are off this planet."

"Let's begin our journey then."

They bought some stallions from a stable in town and road towards the city of Trinity. Anamanto loped easily beside the mounted party members on long Votea legs. It was two more earth days until their next stop. But here it was nothing but a hot day with no moons scheduled to block the sun.

I assume, said Az to his horse stuck in his own mind on the journey with nothing to do but think, *that when you are forever, things don't need to be done quickly.*

The trees here alone can make you feel old; however, travelling among them feels as though they drain the age away and replenish the soul with new energy. Wouldn't you say my friend?

The horse simply kept walking.

He looked at Brial.

"It feels as though I've been here a hundred years already, and yet when I look into the eyes of the people around me, it is as if they see right through me. As if my soul is too young to have burned a hole into the presence of existence. And when I look around at everyone on this road, it is as if the people move past us, too wrapped up in their own lives to see what is around them or even notice we are here. I wonder how long it was that I lived like them."

Brial looked back at Az with wonder. "Azuse, look at that Votea. He thinks you are worth guarding and would now kill all of us to protect you. You are not as young and naive as you lead on to be."

9

Trinity

When they finally reached Trinity, there was a giant termite hill climbing out from the side of a mountain made of some kind of rock plaster with a core of metal as though a meteor of metals, fused together by an ancient explosion, plunged deep into the planet before blanketing itself again with the rubble. The city around it had what looked like tall smokestacks in front of the mountain with stairs running along the outside of them made of the same material. While looking up at the walls of the city and the termite skyscrapers, Az remembered what Nagi had once said.

> *Cities are forever at war with one another. When one group of life becomes too great in numbers, they expand. Usually outwards instead of up, and therefore, into neighbouring lands. However, if those neighbouring*

> lands do not accept them, or their ideas are different, or the neighbouring land is overpopulated too, then it is war.
>
> War will decrease the population so that the land can produce the needs to sustain a lower population of life, and one race is either enslaved to feed the other race or they trade knowledge and resources. Either way, as long as nukes or chemicals are not involved, which they do not use here, with a lowered population, it becomes a golden age for a time. That is until greed has its way again.

The Golden Kings, Az, and Anamanto walked through the front gates into the city of Trinity, the city of the Kamikiri. If there was one thing all cities did it was pride themselves on the grandness of their entrances, and there always seemed to be three spikes on the wall in front of the city. It's just that these spikes had heads on them.

The first immortal, Talah, pointed to the heads.

"You see the spikes, Az? In each city, if there is a problem, the root of that problem is always tracked down into three main people, the hydra snake. Once you have cut off all three heads, you have killed the beast. But, if you only cut off one or two, then it will grow into five more heads. It is an action that takes years of investigating and less than a day to execute."

Once they entered the city, Anamanto—one of the Votea race that served the gods and who was older than all of mankind on Earth—went into the temple of the Cham Shan. The kings went to the bar, and Az wandered through a market that had the smell of opened sewers beneath it. But the contrast of living and cooked animals made him hungry.

He sat down at a vendor and pointed to the coffee and plate of meat that the Kamikirian beside him was eating. The termite behind the counter said something to him, Az just nodded and was handed a plate of food with a cup of coffee. Man did he ever love that smell of coffee.

He pushed the eyeballs to the side of the plate, grabbed the meat with his fingers, and ate some.

"Not bad", he said to the Kamikirian beside him, "but, the coffee tastes a little like mud." The creature just snorted and kept eating as though Az was not even there.

He sat there eating and watched the man behind the counter of the stand. He would scrape the leftover food out onto a pile on the ground to be eaten by a large sluglike thing.

They stood on long back legs and had smaller legs at their midriff—or perhaps they were a second pair of arms—and primary arms higher up on their torsos. Their faces sported long twitching whiskers that suggested they were creatures who evolved in dark tunnels once.

He watched what the thing next to him paid with, and Az copied, paying with a copper lepta. Then he left and wandered around the market a bit more until he returned to the bar.

He walked in from the bright street to the dark room and saw Brial sitting at the bar just inside the door. When he saw Az, he motioned him over.

"Come on, I'll buy you a drink. You know, with age comes less of a need to wander from a place that has all you need."

Az sat down at the bar next to him, and they drank a dozen or so warm flat ales in copper cups—this to keep them from being smashed and having to be replaced like the clay ones no doubt.

Then two Agoti came in and sat at the bar; they giggled while they walked past Brial and Az sitting there. Az turned his head, and his jaw dropped as he turned back to the bar.

"You know, Az, it's said that they can get in your head and even read your mind."

"Then they will know exactly what I am thinking."

"Are you doing this because of them, or because of your trip to the temple and the Agoti there?"

"I guess I will have to find that out then won't I."

He walked up to them while Brial watched as Az's lips moved and theirs didn't—to Az they were talking, and he never even caught on that, to him, they were speaking English.

"Hello ladies, my name is Azuse, but you can call me Az, and your names must be the names of stars, for it looks as though the stars fell from the sky to create such beautiful eyes."

"I am Antisha, and this is my sister Pledrea, you do not seem like you are from here, Azuse."

"No, I am from Earth a planet far from here."

"We know of this blue planet you speak of, human," said Pledrea. "But here is my question for you: Which one of us do you find the most attractive?"

He looked into their eyes as Brial laughed out loud and looked away.

"Your mother must have been an angel for she gave birth to two of the most beautiful daughters."

He could see them start to smile. Travelling for so long can make a man feel so lonely even with his travelling companions. The reason why most people never live past five hundred, travellers either kill themselves after so long on the road or retire early and settle down to raise a family taking on a boring desk job somewhere if they cannot retire, and most women a man will meet on the road will only talk to men they already know.

"Then tell me this, Azuse, which one of us do you like?" Pledrea asked him with a smirk grin.

Az knew he had been in this trap question before, and to him, there was no right answer as he considered returning to his barstool before he made a bigger fool out of himself. Antisha giggled and looked down.

"You are pure and beautiful Pledrea, but Antisha is the one that I would like to know more."

Pledrea moved over a stool leaving a spot between her and Antisha. "Why don't you buy us a drink so we can talk some more?"

Drink followed drink followed drink, as they talked about nothing and talked some more. Pledrea, at one point, told her sister she would see her at home, and after a few more drinks Antisha asked Az if he would walk her home.

They walked down the cobblestone road, and he caught her just as she lost her footing and was about to fall. She giggled and leaned into his arm the rest of the way as they came to a house with only one light on.

He leaned in for a long kiss goodbye, and she asked him if he had a place to stay during the moonlight. He shrugged his shoulders, and she asked him to come inside. When he woke up, they were laying side by side. He had his right arm over her and she had his left under her head as she began to move her hips before rolling over for a kiss.

As they lay there, they knew it was time for him to go. He kissed her once more before he put on his clothes.

Antisha looked at him. "I would ask if you would stay, but then you are a soldier, and although you think you are doing all of this of your own free will, you will always complete your mission until you are killed by one. Even if you were to stay, the fates would find a way for you to leave again, Azuse."

"I will see you again one day, Antisha. You will see."

She got up and walked naked to a chest of drawers and pulled out a silver necklace. On it was a small clenched silver fist that held what looked like a dragon or serpent with red eyes. She clasped it around his neck and looked him in the eyes.

"I know you will," she said.

As he walked out the door, Antisha held her stomach. When he had gone, she closed the door with a soft click. Each step he took, he wanted to turn back. He walked past a shop that had stairs going down with a red carpet and a smell that was all too familiar to him.

He tipped the man at the door a silver obol, and a termite brought him to a bed carved into the wall. He sat on it, and another brought a tray with a lit candle and what looked like hash and opium. He pointed to some of the tar and handed it a silver obol. It gave him a pipe and lit a small stick that it put at the end of the pipe. Az inhaled the darkness and slid down so he was laying on the bed. Thoughts of Antisha soon slipped from his head.

He was now back at Nagi's cave, walking along the glowing rocks as if his feet were not moving and he were just floating. As he floated down the stairs to the bookshelf with the apple on it, he put the book of Adam into his bag. Then all the doors in the house slammed shut at once, and he woke up to see Brial and Klotzen standing over him.

"You have been gone for some time now, I had a feeling this is where we would find you," said Brial.

Klotzen handed him a small leather book bag that was on the bed beside him. "Come on, Az, everyone is waiting for us back at the bar."

Az, still in a haze from what happened, did not remember walking into the place with a bag. But he did remember it from his dream. Perhaps he was mistaken.

–Life Is a Stage

When they got to the bar, Nilhal and Anamanto were standing at the door, and the rest of the Kings of Origon were sitting inside.

Nilhal smiled. "We were wondering if you were going to come back when we heard you left with the telepaths."

Then Anamanto turned and looked into the bar. "It is time to go!"

The kings looked at each other, shrugged, and nodded. Then they all walked out the door into the sunlight and heat again. Az looked down the street in the direction of Antisha's place as they walked in the other direction. He did not speak for several Earth days. He just looked at people's faces as they walked by.

They decided to take him to a concert to try and cheer him up. Even Anamanto insisted on catching a concert at the amphitheatre, and Az thought about how he was just too busy to go to one with Nagi.

They sat in the middle row, far enough from the front, but close enough that they could still see the stage. There were three conductors standing on the stage, and just as it began, a loud bass noise echoed, and a cascade of different colour light beams came shooting from the stage in front of the conductors to the ceiling. The three conductors synchronized their movements by putting their hands over one colour blocking it from reaching the dome over them. As the light stream was broken, a bass noise came. As they moved their hands closer to the audience, breaking more colours, the sound became sharper. Az noticed that the colours that were darkest were closest to the conductors, and lighter colours were closer to the audience.

When the darker colours were broken, a deeper bass would sound, and the lighter the colour the higher pitched the note was. Each colour was like hitting a different key on a keyboard. There were so many colours and shades on the stage, it took three of them to reach one side to the other. Half way through the show, they brought three more conductors to the stage to work the lighter colours in front.

Soon the sound became more than just sound, it became emotions and not sounds at all. Anamanto leaned down to Az.

"This is the song of creation."

Az's mind was no longer in his body. He lifted from it, floating looking down at the audience, feeling like the colours reflecting on the top of the dome. He could see it was not just the sound that was hypnotizing—the colours remaining were blending together, creating a contradiction between the eyes and the mind as the light encased the bodies. Az could not just stay there now without the trappings of pain, and he knew its use was to hold the soul in place. He was now free to travel from the trappings of the body. He shot up out of the planet and into the galaxy as though his mind could see all and nothing at once. Then as he felt the absolute power—as though he could control it all if he stayed there—he returned back to his body again.

When it was over, Az turned to the others.

"That was beautiful. It was as if they were making wind, and the wind was colour, and the colour was my soul taking in life again."

They left the theatre along with countless other people back into the city again.

"So how much further until the mountains?" Az asked.

"It will be a few more moons until we even get out of the city," said Nilhal.

But with the heat and the smell of open sewers, it all quickly became unbearable. However, they pressed on, there was nothing else they could do. As a wise man once said so long ago: "If you're going through hell, keep going."

Brial said, "There is a path through the mountains that the city is cut into. It will lead us to the valley of the dead that will take us to *Cronus*. After the god was buried, all the kings on this entire continent took up the theory that they must be buried in large tombs in the valley *Cronus* was imprisoned in because, some day, he would break free and bring the dead back to life, freeing them from hell."

They gathered supplies before they left the city towards the mouth of the large cave. The tunnel had many steel tracks for bringing metals out from the hills but no dirt. They were able to purchase a ride on one of them for some jerked meat and three skins of water. The termite pushed the bucket until it began to move on its own down a gentle slope. Soon they were deep inside of the cave where a lift took the full buggies up to another path that Az figured led back to the front on a slope. They exited the buggy, and the termite began to fill it up again. At one of the stations, Az looked at the ten kings as they walked—none of them ever really talked. They just walked staring with their glassy eyes as if nothing were around them and nothing ever changed.

"We will stop at the market," Brial said, "to gather the rest of the food and water we will need to finish this journey."

For four days they travelled through the dark tunnels until they reached the market in the middle of the cave. It was a huge circled room with countless tunnels along the walls leading everywhere. It was all lit by the copper lining the walls, giving a green glow that was fueled by fermented fruits, a kind of wine in copper basins. Just like what the US army had found in the ancient ruins in Baghdad during the twenty-first century—an artifact that was termed the "Baghdad battery."

The market was an intriguing place that sold mining tools, ropes, lanterns, crude iron ores, all different metals, food, gems, and diamonds.

"You see this is where you purchase the metals and then pick them up outside," Brial said. "However, only the Kamikiri are allowed in here, so you must have one of them represent you here to do your purchasing."

"If that's the case," Az said, "then why are we allowed in?"

"Because when we first landed, no one was allowed in this city of any race but the Kamikiri. So we invaded the city. With their control of the metals and greed of the banking system, they could only hire mercenaries to come at us, and by the time an army from other cities were persuaded in fighting for them, we had full control over Trinity. Then we broke it off into shares from all the other opposing cities willing to join us."

"So, you enslaved them?"

"No, Az. The cost of the metals jumped to the point that the Kamikiri still made the same amount of money for their services. Only now, the flow is controlled to the other cities by the other cities and it has allowed us a representative in all cities and a say in the state affairs on the mainland. There are two ways to fight a war, with blood or with money, and an invading army can just as easily buy what they are after rather than take it by force if the price is right."

Az could not help but wonder if the Kamikiri had been digging this mine for so long their bodies adapted to look like that, or if they looked like that first.

"Can we rest here a bit?" asked Az.

"It's best not to rest where you are not welcome," said Brial. "Individually they can be controlled, but as a mass they are anarchists."

Az saw a box of what looked like beef jerky as they passed the stands, and he grabbed two handfuls. The price was incredibly high—six times higher than the price outside the caves. The Kamikiri behind the table weighed them, and Az paid then filled his inside pocket with them.

They walked through the rest of the cave, knowing that Anamanto instilled enough fear to ensure they were not bothered.

At the other side of the mountain, the Kamikiri were dumping the buckets of dirt onto a large screen and were shoveling it around. The buckets were dumped onto the first coarse screen and the material would fall through to the next finer screen, then the next, then the next. Whatever couldn't be broken up for the next screen was placed into buckets that were dumped into piles and examined. The metal was shovelled back into buckets and carried back into caves and the dirt was then filtered one more time on a huge screen under a small waterfall coming from the top of the mountain. This process washed away the dirt into the river, leaving any smaller metal or gem left behind to be gathered up.

"And what of all the dirt flowing into the river?" asked Az.

"There are huge dams," said Brial. "Once the swamp is full of life and seaweed at the other end, the water is drained, and the land is farmed, and when the farming has taken all of the nutrients from the soil, it is refilled and another swamp drained. It is a balance that is kept to preserve the viability of the soil and sustain the life of many cities. The food is actually more important than the precious metals."

Az thought about that before he replied. "So what once was barren land now feeds many."

After standing there a few hours, watching the workers, a barge could be seen on the river being pulled across by a rope stretched from one embankment to another. They paid a fee to the Kamikiri and walked onto the barge that took them across the river and into the desert lands.

Now on the other side, they rested under the shade of a giant rock giving their eyes and minds time to recover from the dark. They stayed along the riverbank for two moons while they broke bread, fished, and drank wine they had purchased in the caves before they had crossed the river.

10

Cronus Prison

Az awoke on the bank of the river during dusk on the third moon with that hazy feeling where you do not know if it's real or still a dream. He gazed along the final path they were to follow out of hell—so close and yet so far away. Each day the same, and at the end—if there is an end—then what? Another mission, then one more after that. Like that last drink on a Friday night, that's never enough (and too much the next day). Until you wonder if there is anything left. Anything left inside. Any strength left to live. Was the body now just a husk holding what little remains of the soul awaiting the day to die?

As they walked through the valley of the dead, there was one symbol they continued to see; it was carved into rock, painted on stone, or made with pebbles into the sand. It was a circle with a line—the big dipper pointing at the North Star.

To be alive during that time, a race would have to be hundreds of thousands of years old.

The valley of the dead was surrounded by mountains where, with the passing of every moon blocking the sun, Sirius would touch the peaks in the distance. Eventually, they were close enough to see that it only touched one of the mountain peaks. That was how they kept on track with every moon as they walked through the valley, through the sun, the heat, the day, the light, the night, through the smell of burning flesh, over charred bones. And the dangers did not end there.

There were exiles due to disease and plague with bandits and tomb robbers hiding everywhere. There were countless tiny pyramid tombs scattered along the landscape. Some were turned into houses and others into new graves. The more they walked, the closer the tombs became to one another, until it felt like they were walking through a necropolis or city of the dead.

With unseen eyes peering out from the darkness of the tombs, no one talked, no one dared to. The kings all held the grips of their swords, and Anamanto carried his enormous staff with both hands.

Az kept his right hand on his sidearm, but after a few hours, began to let his guard down. It was a good thing no one else did because, as soon as he took his hand off it, to hold the back of his head and stretch, out from the tombs they came. Az started shooting, but quickly ran out of ammo. As a sword passed by his head, he grabbed the arms of the bandit whose face had been painted to look like a skull and whose mouth had been stitched shut.

Anamanto smashed down on its head, staving its skull in, and Az picked up the sword and began to hack body parts onto the ground. The kings and Az circled the Votea who took his staff into the air and went down on one knee banged the bottom of the staff onto the ground so hard the echo rang in their ears. As the top of the staff opened, a red beam of light shot out from it in all directions over their heads. The beam then spun until it looked like a solid circle in front of the kings, and when it hit the bandits, the immense heat caused them to burst into flames as it shot right through them. In little more than a second, there was nothing but ash left of the attackers.

"Let's hope that will be the last of them," said Anamanto. "The staff will take until the next moon to charge."

They continued on walking for many moons until one night, by moonlight, they stopped at a large stone circle surrounded by large pillars.

Brial pointed at the stone. "Look Az, it is a map of the stars long before our kind even came up with the knowledge again to reach the stars. It's like a stamp with the date in it."

"From back when the gods were feared and worshiped," said Anamanto.

"Before their cruelty as well," said Az.

"Ahhh right," said Anamanto. "So much better than the one god you bow down to."

"No, our one God is not a god at all. It is one because it is one power in all, one force that brings everything together. It is all at once and yet nothing at all, it is one we can control as it also controls us. While we use it, and it uses us, it is the power from the universes and existence itself. It is in you and me, in that rock, that cloud, that sun, all of the moons. It was there before the beginning, it is here now, and it will be with us after the end."

"Our power," said Anamanto, "comes from our lives, the lives of our ancestors, and the collective life of all that has ever originated from Enif, our home world. You would know this if your kind came from a planet and not a lab where you were pulled away from your true mother planet."

"Come on you guys," said Talah, "without a drink in my hand there is no point in discussing religion."

As they went to walk away, Az just kept staring at a circle.

"Wait, you guys, what does that symbol in the middle mean?"

He pointed to what looked like a mathematical equation inside of it. The image burned into his mind to write it out as soon as he had his next T2700.

"I don't know," said Brial, "these old ruins are full of forgotten knowledge."

Then they walked over the circle towards the mountains and did not think twice about it.

When they reached the base of the mountain, there was a path with stairs that stretched to the clouds themselves. Each step was carefully notched into the side of the mountain to be exactly like the one before it. To climb down would be easy, if you did not fall, but the climb up would be exhausting.

When they finally reached the top, there was a large corridor cut into the peak of the mountain with two beautiful statues of women with their breasts showing at the entrance.

"The mothers of man," said Anamanto. "The protectors of the gods, and the wives of Orion—there to ensure only the pure blood of the gods are allowed to pass into the Halls of the Gods.

Who is going to pass through, who thinks they are worthy to walk in the hall of thunder?"

Az stepped forward. "I'll go!"

"I'll accompany you," said Brial.

And with that they both began to walk between the statues.

Az could feel an uncanny shiver creep across the flesh between his shoulder blades. Brial felt nothing, no emotions whatsoever—for him every step was like the one before it. When they were directly between the statues, the heads of the statues turned so they were facing them, then red beams shot out from their eyes. Brial only looked at Az.

"Goodbye, my friend."

As the beams scorched Brial to ash, he never made a sound, if a thought ran through his head in the final second of his existence, it did not show on his face. He was simply no more. But as the beams came at Az, the eyes of the serpent in the clenched fist of his medallion lit up, creating a shield around him.

Az kept walking. When he'd passed beyond the deadly gaze of the statues and into the large hall, he turned back and looked at Anamanto and the nine remaining Kings of Origon, standing there staring at him. Then he heard voices that sounded like a song hummed by women, and it was as if the song were guiding his next move. He plucked the now writhing serpent from the medallions grip. It grew and slid around his wrist and hardened again.

As though the humming was the air itself, he felt it like the soft embrace of a woman guiding his movements and an uncanny feeling that he had been there before. He walked over to one of the guardian statues, guided by the mysterious humming that felt like it was controlling his movements as long as he did not fight it and placed the now empty silver hand into a small hole in the square base the statue was standing on and turned its wrist three times until a small white crystal emerged from the statue's womb. He took it and placed it into his bag and walked to the other statue and repeated the process. Then the sound stopped, and he signaled for the party to come. All ten started walking at the same time towards the hall. Again, the heads turned to face them. Only this time they did not fire.

Before entering the cave, they stopped and looked at the huge hall. It was a thing of beauty with pillars on both side and statues all around even carved into the walls.

Anamanto looked down at Az.

"Perhaps you are more than just a speck in time?"

They walked through the mighty hall, each step echoed, and small rocks dropped from the ceiling that sounded like thunder when they hit the ground. When they reached the end of the massive hall there was only one side of the ship showing, leaving a door to the hull opened and a round set of stairs made with skulls. Az pondered what they would have done at that point if the door was closed.

Anamanto said, "Those are but some of the people who died when the ship first came here. They were enslaved here to build the cavern."

The party walked up the stairs and into the belly of *Cronus* as though they had already been there.

"I will check the engines," said Anamanto, "and see how they maintained over all this time."

Talah said, "I want to find the controls."

The immortal named Moot went with Talah.

The rest of them split off in twos and searched the ship. Az and Klotzen went wandering around a while until Az found a room with a bed in it.

"Well Klotzen, I will see you later, I am taking some well-needed rest."

"That is fine, I will find the others and let them know."

–The Final Push.

Az awoke for the first times since he was in hell without strange dreams or nightmares in his head. He looked around the room and found himself a black trench coat and clothes that fit him that smelled better than the ones after his long journey.

He ran his fingers through his hair and realized how long it had become along with his beard. He walked out of the room and down the long corridor, occasionally looking in a room. Then he realized the lights were on as he looked up at them. He eventually found his way to the bridge where the immortals were discussing the controls and Az pulled the book with the apple out from his sack.

"Would this help?"

Klotzen looked over the book's pages. "No, not for this, but I know something it will be good for. This ship has a cloning device."

"So, what are you suggesting?" said Az.

Talah was nodding. "We storm the city of Gomorrah using it and re-forge the Golden Sword."

"It would be the only way they would leave," said Klotzen.

"What do you mean?" said Az.

Talah explained. "The rest of the immortals created a huge city called Gomorrah with a massive army by the ocean. The Ships of the Gods do not carry armies. They carry flight crews and only clone massive armies to take over the planets for them, using the people from the planet to clone. It looks like this book has the formulas including how to map the chemical compounds of the brain to imprint the necessary memories and ideas needed for war and many other functions."

And how does the planet support such a massive increase in life?" Az asked.

"It doesn't," said Talah. "The cloned troops are sterile and die off within a couple of weeks, it's part of the genetic programming. Long enough to achieve any victory with that many disposable troops."

"I don't believe it," Az said. "Our human armies with free will and thought to choose their own paths would destroy this mindless monstrosity of life. Time and time again."

"Well," said Anamanto, "I think you will be given the chance to put your words to the test, human!"

Az just nodded at the towering Votea and looked back at Talah.

"How does Gomorrah pay for such a large army," Az asked. "Is it a slave army?"

Talah shook her head. "The salt. The city supplies it to the entire mainland. If you control the city, you control the salt, and the armies are paid in salt, most of the food is preserved with salt. If you hold Gomorrah, you are already in control of the mainland."

"I see," said Az. "So whose DNA are we going to clone?"

"Yours, of course," said Talah. "Our DNA is too corrupted after all these years. Yours is still pure and full of flavour."

Nilhal winked at Az and laughed. "Come on, let's go."

Klotzen and Nilhal went with Az to the cloning chambers. They could feel *Cronus* lifting out from its mountain prison. As it lifted and propelled forward, the massive ship clipped the top of a mountain and over the intercom came the voice of Anamanto.

—You humans never could learn how to fly—

The Votea helped navigate the ship to Origon where they landed it on the huge front courtyard dwarfing the little ship beside it. Sixty immortals were all that was left along with the ten kings (now nine) who did not choose to leave and live in the luxury of Gomorrah where their every need was met. The loading door opened just under the cloning tanks. It took six days to clone an army of 50,000 soldiers that would walk out those doors.

The immortals loaded the ship with supplies and began the terra growing projects in the ship. The Ships of the Gods had growing rooms for food and other needs like herbs as well as rooms for raising livestock. It was the reason for always finding a bio-footprint on any planet the gods visited, like opium, and coffee. Earth's first ships to the Alpha Centauri systems, the Babylon fleets, had the same type of idea with its own grow rooms to support life and oxygen on the ships. It had six flight crews to be thawed out one by one as the one before it retired. Then once on Proxima b, the human eggs would be fertilized for the population. At that time, each family or corporation was responsible for paying for the fertilization and transport to the planet.

Of course, the first ship to go there never even made planetfall and created a spaceport where the colony stayed. It was still in use as a defensive perimeter, and Earth would later take that method and do what it does best, mass produce and keep sending more ships now that they had a half way point to stop at. But once Earth learned of the magnetic bridges between systems and the dark matter that connected each sun to one another, the ships Earth sent later, on the magnetic bridges could hold all the supplies it would need, and it was decided the space for the grow rooms was not necessary, and Earth's fleets became more military than exploratory.

The immortals landed *Cronus* two days out from Gomorrah. It was more like jumping the ship then flying it. The cloning feeding tubes were unhooked from the army, their belly buttons were cauterized, and they were sent to war lead by Klotzen Gabriel Herrmann.

Az felt the scar on his belly from his old combat suit's waste tube and wondered just how different the human army now was from the gods' army.

The clones stormed the city walls with great fury, killing everyone they could, and Klotzen stood on the wall of the city but never even received a scratch. Every seventh day, another wave was thrown at Gomorrah's walls. Six days to clone and one day to clean the machines and ensure the crops were pure.

It went on like this for several Earth months. The Golden Army stayed in their towers, watching their citizens being slaughtered until the city was nothing more than fire and rubble. All that remained were the two huge towers in the middle of Gomorrah that stood watch over the city.

Nemth and Halmita, the tenth immortal, left the ship and walked the two-day journey through the rubble that had been Gomorrah. They walked amongst the huge clone army surrounding the tower and breathed the smell of dead or burning bodies and the bloating dying clone soldiers who lay rotting at their feet. Nemth and Halmita stood at the entrance of the tower until a large man with three chins came out to talk to them, wearing a toga.

It was Glaxnox, the second in command to Nemth during the age of the Golden Army. He walked out alone and stopped when he was face to face with Nemth.

"Why have you come to my city, Nemth? You know with but a wave of my hand I could have unleashed the Golden Army on these *things*, and they would have been no more."

Nemth just pointed to the sky. As Glaxnox looked up, the sky above them changed into purple, red, and blue that blocked out the sun. That was when *Cronus* began to land again on the rubble.

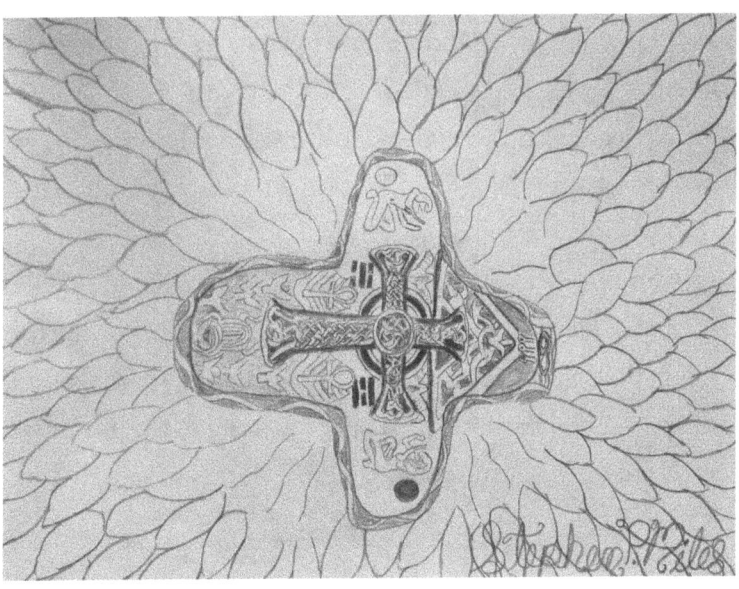

After it landed, the immortals walked out from the ship lead by Talah and stood by Nemth. Then Glaxnox signaled for the rest of them to come out from the towers, and Az watched from the ship as the Golden Army, wearing extravagant robes, walked out from their towers. They came together in a row two-by-two, and as they met up with the others that were standing behind Nemth and the nine kings on both sides of him, it looked as though it was a sword forged onto its grip.

Nemth spoke in a commanding voice, and his words echoed between the two towers. "It is time to leave this planet. There is a new war, the end war, the war we have been waiting for."

They loaded onto the ship and lifted off up into the outer atmosphere, bringing with them a huge wave onto the shore. Az was in the war room with Anamanto as they got ready to drop a liquid hydrogen bomb that would leave no trace that the city ever existed.

"We cannot drop it when we are still in the atmosphere," said Anamanto. "Or it will drain too much of our shield strength, and we could breach the hull."

And so, just as the ship entered the orbit, the Votea dropped the liquid hydrogen bomb on the rubble of the city. It liquefied the tower and rock into lava and turned the sand to glass—and transformed people watching in the distance to perfect statues of ash that looked like pillars of salt.

This book is dedicated to the memory of my grandfather Frank Simmons.

They say that when you start to write a story you should write about what you know. I grew up hearing a story about how my grandfather was working in a coal mine in northern Canada and when they offered him to fight in the war he said "Anything would be better than this." This was before D-Day, and there was a mission to destroy cannons that were three storeys tall so that the boats could land on the beaches of Normandy. The fact that he was Canadian, and the other soldier who survived was Dutch means one has to assume this was an international mission of whatever soldiers were still on the mainland before D-Day.

I watched history movies for years and never once saw anything about any three-storey cannons that had to be taken out.

That is until around 2017.

I was watching a program on the *History Channel* about V1 rockets that were dug into the ground and had a length of a three-storey building. In the documentary, they said that the Germans never had these working, and that if they had, then D-Day could have never happened. But that is not the story I grew up hearing.

In the version I heard, the three-storey cannons *were* operational and had to be taken out *before* D-Day. Also, only my grandfather and the youngest soldier survived to make it back to Britain so that the D-Day landings could take place— he later landed on the beaches of France with the men of

D-Day. There was also another time, my grandmother told me my grandfather was upset because he was watching an old documentary of D-Day featuring footage of the camera crew he was with, and it was like he was there again. Back then, they were not filming that war because they wanted to make a documentary one day.

There was also one more story whose details I was too young to know from my grandfather. It involved Allied captains drinking in a captured town and how my grandfather asked about sneaking off to the wine cellar with his chum. When he awoke, everyone was dead, and the town had been taken over by Germans. The Allies would take a town over by day. But the Germans got really good at reclaiming them at night.

I never got to know the details of that story because my grandfather died while I was too young to care. But somehow my grandfather and one other person who woke up in that wine cellar took back the town and captured a bunch of the Germans defending it.

These stories became very important to me.

Written in Mexico by Stephen P. Miles – Canadian

www.ingramcontent.com/pod-product-compliance
Lightning Source LLC
LaVergne TN
LVHW021715060526
838200LV00050B/2680